Finch Books by J.S. Frankel:

The Menagerie

THE MENAGERIE

J.S. FRANKEL

The Menagerie
ISBN # 978-1-78651-880-4
©Copyright J.S. Frankel 2016
Cover Art by Posh Gosh ©Copyright March 2016
Interior text design by Claire Siemaszkiewicz
Finch Books

Published in 2016 by Finch Books Newland House, The Point, Weaver Road, Lincoln, LN6 3QN, United Kingdom.

THE
MENAGERIE

Dedication

To my wife and children, for they make every day of the week my greatest adventure, and to animal lovers everywhere.

Chapter One
Memories of days past

Karen Fox rubbed her right leg—the bad one—sighed, and figured that she might as well get out of bed. Hospital beds weren't all that comfortable, so she turned over onto her left side, slid out of bed and stood up. She gripped the cool tiles with her toes while she teetered unsteadily for a moment. Once she regained her balance, she limped over to the window. Scents of summer—fir and pine trees, hollyhocks and azaleas—drifted in through the window along with the sounds of shouting. She muttered, "It *would* be a nice day today."

Today was the middle of July, the time was around noon, and although the Portland weather was hot and dry, a cool breeze swirled around her. It was different from the air conditioner. It was natural and pleasant, whereas the air-conditioning unit put out a steady stream of dry air that made her cough. Pleasant or not, it didn't matter. Instead, she shifted her gaze to the sky and prayed for rain.

Since being brought here roughly two months ago, Karen had grown to despise sunny days and hate the summer season. What she hated more than anything was the idea of people going around in shorts and tank tops and riding bikes and everything else sixteen-year-old kids did when they were fully capable.

Now, all the fun of life had been taken away and she just wished—selfishly so—for it to rain and dampen everyone else's fun. Let Mother Nature do her worst and not just rain but storm. Bring on a flood, a volcanic explosion or something else equally dire. If she couldn't enjoy life, why should they?

"Don't be selfish," she whispered a second later, and took back her wish. Thinking about it, it was just plain mean. Even if life didn't work the way she wanted it to, she couldn't go around blaming anyone for what had happened. Part of her said that it would be fun. Everyone deserved a little misery in their lives. However, the other part, the rational and decent part, said no.

"Hey, what's up, Megan?"

The question floated up to Karen's position, and she followed the source. There, a few people she knew from her school rode by and she moved away from the window, flattening her back against the wall. Doubtful they saw her, as she was on the second floor, and who looked up while riding along, anyway?

After sneaking a peek, she saw their bicycles disappear down the road and breathed a faint sigh of relief. The breeze blew some strands of her long, dirty blonde hair around her face and she brushed them away with an impatient flick of her hand.

Letting out a series of grunts as she moved back to the bed, she winced with every step. The accident had been a bad one. She'd been in the back seat of her father's car, enjoying the ride and then...then the bright light had come from the onrushing car. She'd heard her mother screaming, her father yelling "Get down!" and the sound of metal being crushed…

* * * *

May fifteenth, two months ago

"You've had an accident," one of the nurses told her in a kindly voice. A middle-aged woman, heavy with a tangle of dyed black hair, she wore a strained smile.

"What happened?"

Karen's first words…accident victims always said that, didn't they? This had been her first real accident. Biking and running and roller skating had always been part of her life. Bruised knees and elbows came with it, but now, this was major, so she asked the obvious question.

The lights in the room were dim and shadows lurked in every corner. Moonlight came through the drawn shades. A smell of antiseptic hung in the cool air and stabs of pain lanced through every fiber of her being. Her right leg hurt and had a heavy cast on it, suspended by a sling that hung from a support bar attached to the bed. Thick bandages had been wrapped around her right forearm. An intravenous tube ran from a bag in an overhead support and fed into the vein in her right arm.

She didn't take much note of that, though. Instead, she focused on the pain. Her right cheek hurt monstrously, and bringing her good arm up to feel her face, her fingers encountered more bandages.

"You were in a car accident," the nurse gravely intoned. "You don't remember it, do you?"

"Not much," said Karen, struggling to think. "Where are my parents?"

"I'm sorry."

Just two words, but they carried a lot of meaning, and the meaning knifed into Karen's head with all the immediacy of a thunderbolt. A second later, the tears began. "I want to see them," she sobbed out. "Where are they?"

As she struggled to get off the bed, the nurse gently pushed her back and said, somewhat reluctantly, "They're...in the morgue. You just had an operation and you need to rest."

"I want to see them!" Karen screamed and once more tried to get up, lashing out with her good arm. Her fist connected with the nurse's cheek. She heard the nurse grunt then another nurse ran in, a needle at the ready. Karen felt it stab her arm then...nothing.

Waking up the next day, pain still there but somewhat more manageable, Karen noticed the sun streaming in and she felt a little stronger. The nurse whom she'd belted walked in with a massive bruise on her cheek, but a professional smile in place. "Are you feeling better?"

"Yes." Karen nodded and mentally steeled herself for what she was going to ask and what she had to see. "I'm sorry about hitting you."

The nurse inclined her head slightly. "You were upset. I understand."

It was good that someone understood. "Can I...see my parents now?" Karen asked in a faint voice.

"I'll get the doctor."

Long story short, the doctor—a reed-thin man somewhere in his fifties—took her in a wheelchair down to the morgue. Along the way, he said that his name was Doctor Jensen. She had to be strong. There was nothing that anyone could have done, and once she saw the words Hospital Mortuary, she choked up and began to sob once more.

There they lay on separate tables. Karen's tears fell faster when she saw the bodies of her parents lying still and quiet, cried some more as she touched her mother's face and begged her to wake up, all the while knowing that her mother would never wake again, then the doctor wheeled her back to her room. There, the nurse helped her into bed.

"What happened?" Karen asked after she'd semi-composed herself.

"You had a very bad accident," Doctor Jensen said, taking a chair and sitting next to the bed. "Your right leg was shattered, and we're worried that there might be some nerve damage. We're not sure yet. You have major abrasions on your right forearm, and you might have a slight concussion. You also lost a lot of blood. Things were touch-and-go for a while, but we got you back."

Facts given and manner grave, he got up from the chair and delivered his prognosis. "You're young. You'll heal. In time, you'll be capable of doing most things."

Going over to the door, he turned back with a somber expression on his face. "I'm truly sorry about your parents."

With that, he walked out, and feeling totally bereft, Karen began to cry all over again. Capable, she'd be capable of doing most things, the doctor had said.

Capable…she hated that word. It implied that if one was not capable, then they were no one. She suspected that in spite of all the rehab they had planned, in spite of all the water walking and weight training to come, in spite of all that and the fact that she was young, she wouldn't be all that capable.

A couple of days later, she got the details from the police, and they placed the blame squarely on the young driver who'd decided to get drunk, hop in his car and cruise at a hundred miles per hour down the highway. "He got drunk. He went too fast, and he lost control," said the policeman, who came in to fill in the missing pieces.

That was it, eleven words summing up the death of her parents. Blame it on the same kind of moron who decided to speed up, like he was thinking, "I can handle it!" and stepped on the accelerator, jumped the concrete divider, and slammed into her parents' car at high speed, killing them in a flash, just like that, and trapping her in the back seat, her right leg crushed and broken into something resembling a jigsaw puzzle...

* * * *

Present day

A stab of agony in her leg brought her back to reality. And the reality was that staying in a hospital was on the high side of dull. School had let out for the summer. After the accident, one of her teachers had brought her homework in at the beginning of each week and each week Karen finished it off in two days. "Well, I'm on vacation," she muttered to the wall as she shut her notebook for the final time. "What do I do now?"

Vacation...some of the girls she knew in school used the word 'vacay' and she found that so pretentious. They could have their 'vacay' — and what did she have? Not very many people had come around to visit. Her teachers had summer vacation, her so-called friends did as well, and that was how life went.

As for rehab, it sucked in the worst way. It hurt, too, but she put up with it. Still, after therapy, what else was there? Television bored her. She didn't care much for music outside of a few bands, and she refused to reread her textbooks. All of this added up to a huge bowl of boring.

"You don't have any family?" the policemen had asked her during her first few days here. "The way I see it, you're underage, and you need a guardian."

A large man, round-faced, stolid and unsmiling, he hadn't sounded unkind. For Karen, she'd figured this was just part of his job, laying down the facts one, two, three then going on to another case, another person, more facts then home, perhaps, to his family. *He* probably had a family. Right now, she'd had her life and only that.

"No, sir," she'd finally said, fighting back the memory of being part of a family one minute and not being part of one a few seconds later. "My grandparents are gone — both sides of my family — and my father never said he had any brothers or sisters. My mother has a sister, but she lives in Europe. She married a guy from Italy."

The policeman had written everything down, and had said he'd get someone from Social Services to come around. "I know you've had a bad time," he'd said, rising from his chair. "But you'll need someone to help you out. I'll see what I can do."

"I could use some more clothes," she'd said. "I, uh…don't have much to wear."

After giving her a friendly nod, he'd walked out. A short time later, a policewoman — young, and with an earnest look about her — had come to the hospital. "I went to your house," she'd said, proffering a bag. "I just took whatever was in the top drawer. Going naked isn't the hottest idea, even though it's summer."

"Thanks," Karen had said softly.

As she looked at the clothes spread out on her bed, depression set in. Wearing sweat pants, hoodies and long-sleeved shirts wasn't her idea of decent fashion.

Pulling the waistband away from her body, she focused her gaze on her withered leg. They'd taken the cast off a week ago. Her right thigh looked to be two inches smaller than her left one, but that didn't bother her as much as the scar. It was a livid thing of stitches and holes and scar tissue, and it ran from the top of her hip down to her knee. Maybe long pants weren't such a bad idea. Same deal with long sleeves. They hid the marks of trauma.

They couldn't hide the memories, though, of having a family then suddenly being an orphan. It was a sudden shift that told her nothing was permanent. The only things that seemed to be permanent were the scars.

The word capable echoed through her mind again. She examined every line and massaged the muscles in her thigh daily, willed them to work and hoped that the rehab and exercise program would set things right.

Bottom line—nothing had changed very much at all. She still limped. At times she couldn't feel her leg and experienced tingling in her right arm. Doctor Jensen had said that she might have damage and it might be permanent. She didn't know if it would ever go away.

Even worse was when she looked in the mirror. A person could always hide their arms and legs. In her case, she couldn't hide her face—not unless she wore a mask, and only superheroes and criminals did that. Along with her leg and arm, the right side of her face had received a deep laceration and her right cheekbone had been shattered in the accident.

A vivid scar remained, running from the edge of her eye three inches down to meet the corner of her mouth, and it twisted the right side of her face up into a horrid half-smile. Say hello to the Joker.

"We can talk to a surgeon about getting rid of that scar," one of the nurses told her. "You shouldn't have to go through life, er…looking like that."

The nurse meant well, but the mirror told Karen the truth. In her mind she looked grotesque. Who would be interested in her now? It wasn't like she was Ms. Popular at school or that many of the guys had spoken with her. One candidate — Jim Caldwell, a guy from the football team — had come around, once. He'd taken one look at her, mumbled something about practice and cut out.

Sure, looks didn't matter. Beauty's only skin deep. She told herself the same story and figured that sooner or later she'd believe it, but it was the mirror — always the mirror — that spoke the real truth, and the real truth was bitterness personified.

The image of a young teen, five-nine and slender and just out of awkward adolescence, stared back at her. With a mane of blonde hair framing a narrow face and a long, aquiline nose, she'd been called plain by some, pretty by others, but right now she forced out a thought that looks didn't matter much.

Or did they? Karen was a solid A student, but who cared about grades? Everyone wanted to hang with the cool kids, the athletic and good-looking kids. The scar threw the whole symmetry of her face off. In a burst of optimism, she hoped that the doctors would perform surgery and she'd look normal one day. She didn't care if she looked like a fashion model. She just wanted to look like everyone else.

Heaving in a deep breath, the thought of *no, I'll never look normal* ran through her mind at light speed and tears once again trickled down the side of her face. If unhappiness could be summed up in a mark, then the scar gave her away along with the haunted look in her eyes. Ordinarily a deep and lush jade green, they now had a smudge of black in them, a touch of death brought on by her brush with the Grim Reaper, a souvenir of the near hereafter.

A knock at the door made her turn around. Ron Goodman, a classmate of hers, stood at the door, a look of uncertainty on his face. He held a bag in his right hand. "Can I come in?" he asked.

Karen didn't know him very well, but during school they occasionally spoke to each other about the mundane facts of scholastic life. She immediately turned the scarred side of her face away while waving him in and walking back to her bed. Along the way she thought twice about her greeting. "Hi," she said, mustering up some friendliness. "It's cool. Come in."

She wore a pair of pink pajamas and was sweaty and tired, but a visitor was a visitor. She hadn't seen anyone for the longest time.

"I, uh… I'm sorry I didn't come around before," he began. "I heard about the accident, but, uh…some of the other kids said you didn't want to see anyone."

Talk about a bullcrap story. They didn't want to see The Scar. Karen thought about tossing off an angry retort, but instead reined in her anger and said, "I guess they were busy."

Ron walked over to the bed, put down the bag and pulled up a chair to sit on. Once seated, he craned his neck over to look at the mark on her face. Karen met his eyes. "Yeah, it's pretty big," she said, trying not to lose it in front of him. "What do you think?"

He offered a shrug. "It's just a mark," he said in an offhand manner.

The corners of her mouth twitched upward in a brief smile, but then a loud woof sounded from outside and Karen jerked her head up. "What was that?" she asked.

"I thought you might like a visitor."

Ron got up and went to the door, opening it. A massive black Labrador bounded in and sat at Ron's side, panting, its long pink tongue hanging out. "This is my dog, Chocolate," he said. "You like him?"

Karen shied back when the dog ambled over to sniff Karen's hand and subsequently lick it. Ron noticed her reaction and asked, "Something wrong?"

"Uh, no, I'm good," she answered, fighting to keep her voice under control. A stray dog, a German shepherd, had bitten her when she was six. She'd cried at the doctor's office while the doctor had put the stitches in, and had cried some more at home.

The experience had been traumatizing and from that point on, she hadn't wanted to be around any four-legged critters. Right now she had enough trouble dealing with most of the two-legged kind. The hospital staff had been pretty decent for the most part, but they had other patients to see and their own lives to live.

"I, uh…it's not you," Karen finally managed to get out. "I'm not really into pets and all that."

Immediately, Ron got a look of disappointment on his face. "Oh, I didn't know. I'll take him outside."

He pulled on the leash, and the dog got up and followed him out of the room. Ron came in a few seconds later. "He's pretty well-trained, so he'll wait outside." He pointed at the bag. "I got some DVDs and a portable player. I thought you might want to watch a few movies or something."

Karen was sincerely touched by the gesture, but still kept the bad side of her face averted. "Thanks," she said in a faint voice. "I'm…just not into watching anything right now."

Both of them fell silent until Chocolate offered a loud woof from outside that broke the stillness. The noise startled Karen, and she edged up against the headboard.

"I guess he's ready to rumble," she said. It was an old expression, something she'd heard on television a long time ago, and it served as her lame way of continuing the conversation. It wasn't that she didn't want Ron to be here. Short and slender, with a mop of brown hair and mild brown eyes, he came across as a pretty unthreatening guy. "So, um, what's up?"

Ron gulped and asked, "If you don't want to watch anything right now, do you want to play some cards?"

She motioned toward the bed and reached for the deck of cards that sat on the night table. "Have a seat. We can do that. I can show off my magic, too."

Karen knew how to cut the deck with one hand, do other sleight-of-hand tricks, and was deadly at gin rummy. She'd been playing cards since she was little and her parents had never beaten her, not once. Everyone had to have a completely useless talent, she figured. This was hers.

As they played, and as Ron lost hand after hand, he asked, "When are you going to get out of here?"

She shrugged. "I don't know. I guess the people at Social Services are going to set something up." Maybe they would. The policeman had taken down her information, but no one had come around to see her, so call it a double-dunk of life and it sucked. She laid down her cards, another winning hand. "Well, that's fifty million you owe me."

Ron chuckled, but then his mood turned serious. He looked down at the floor and swallowed a few more times before picking his head up and saying, "Listen, if you need someone to talk to, I could come around tomorrow…if you want." He offered a guileless smile.

Touched by his offer, Karen said, not trying to sound too eager, "Yeah, that would be cool. I'd like that."

Suddenly, she yawned. It was only midday, but she felt tired. Ron caught the yawn and got up. "If you have to pass out, I'll, um…get going."

"Guess I need my beauty sleep," she cracked and internally kicked herself. Strike the beauty part.

Before going over to the door, he said, "It was really nice seeing you. I'll… I'll come by tomorrow, same time. I promise."

"I'll be here."

Karen waved goodbye and settled back. At the very least, someone had shown up. Not right away, but he'd come. He had…but, as for the others, yeah, good luck with that.

"We'll see you tomorrow," one of her classmates had said during their first and last visit. Said visit had occurred a week after her accident and subsequent operations.

Tomorrow had turned into the day after tomorrow and the day after that. They'd never come around, and Karen had cried when she realized that no one was coming, no one…until Ron showed…

She blinked…it was dark, and the room lay swathed in shadow. Where had the time gone? While shaking her head and laughing silently at her own lousy trip down memory lane, she heard a noise. It sounded like the bleating of a sheep mixed with the cry of a baby.

The sound came from the forest. Maybe it was an animal giving birth. Not that she knew a lot about it, but she'd watched nature channels before and some animals made strange sounds when pushing out their babies. Still, this was one weird noise.

Glancing at the clock, it read nine-thirty, and the sky was full of bright stars. Good time to stargaze, she thought, as she got dressed in a fresh pair of sweats and a hoodie. As she limped out of the door, down the hallway and past the nurse's station, one of the nurses called out, "Karen, you're not supposed to go outside!"

"I won't go far."

It was only to the forest. She'd scout around, figure out what was making that noise, and come back. Moving slowly, her leg paining her, she entered the forest and crept forward slowly, feeling her way around until her eyes could adjust to the dark.

There...up ahead, something lay on the grass in the middle of a clearing, something white, round...and with five legs. It had five legs.

It had *five* legs? *What is going on here?*

Cautiously, she moved over to the white thing and got her first good look at it. Roughly the size of a Frisbee with five slender legs, it lay on the ground and moaned piteously. It had two eyes, two slits for a nose and tiny, shell-like ears. To her, it resembled a cross between a starfish and a manta ray. "What is this?" she whispered. "This is not..."

Her voice trailed off when she saw something metallic up ahead of her. It looked like a ship. "Oh, crap..." she whispered.

It didn't look like a typical UFO—no round shape and bright lights, and no sounds of five-toned music. Roughly the size and shape of a jet plane, the side panel was open and Karen wondered how it could have landed here without a sound and with no one seeing it. It was a clear night. Surely someone must have seen it.

Still... No, it was sitting here and this white thing had just shown up and how did it get here and it was still moaning and she had to call the police...

Crap, what was she supposed to do? "Okay, okay, calm down." She advanced on the creature, her gaze nervously flicking back and forth from the white thing to the ship.

As for the ship, it gave off a faint hum, and while she was studying the details, the white semi-starfish thing raised its head and moaned piteously. This was just too unreal...but she couldn't leave it. Maybe if she got it back on the ship, someone would take care of it. Yeah, that was the plan.

"Hey, I'm here, okay?" she said, and gently touched the side of the creature. It felt warm, its body firm, and she picked it up and cradled it in her arms. "I'll take you back," she murmured.

It immediately fell silent and cuddled up to her. Its eyes, large and purple with gold specks, shone in the darkness, and for a second she had the absurd notion that this creature thought she was its mother.

Her thoughts of the absurd changed when the ship's hum gave way to a faint whine that got higher the closer she approached. "This...is not good," she murmured, her fear growing.

Still, she couldn't put the creature down now, not when the ship was so close. Just a few more yards, she thought, just a few more. Reaching the ship, she deposited the critter inside and it sat there, blinking at her.

A sudden click made Karen stop dead in her tracks. It came from inside the ship, oldest trick in the book—

number one—and she'd fallen for it. The creature had been bait!

"Crap," she muttered, and started to back out. Too late, though, as a blast of yellow fire came hurtling toward her at light speed and hit her point-blank in the chest. On the way down to the ground, she wondered why this had to happen.

Car accidents were one thing, but getting blasted by an alien? This was too weird. Her face hit the ground, and with the last of her strength, she turned over on her back to look at the sky. Then the stars faded from view and blackness settled over her.

Chapter Two
Welcome aboard

Karen awoke with a splitting headache and a sense of dislocation. Wherever she was and whatever she was in, it was…*moving*. It also seemed to be moving fast, yet there were no speed bumps, no potholes. This had to be the smoothest ride ever.

Darkness surrounded her, and warily she got to her feet, her arms out and feeling around for something—anything—solid. Had someone kidnapped her and tossed her in the back of a truck or a semi? Yeah, that was it. She had to be in the back end of something big, but wouldn't it have crates or a tiny window attached to the front cab?

And there was a different smell in here. It smelled like…animals, but not. Yet the smell of fur and crap wasn't human. It was something gamy, foul—something entirely different than what she was used to smelling and…

"Oh crap," she blurted out as the memory of her last few moments in the forest came back to her. She'd picked up the starfish-ray alien, approached the ship, it had fired something at her and...

"I'm on the ship."

There, she said it, said it aloud as if anyone could hear her, and calling Captain Duh to the rescue, come in, over and out. Of *course* she was on the ship, and it was in motion and therefore she had to be in space. "Freak me out," she muttered.

If these were aliens, then could they breathe oxygen? Maybe they could and maybe not, but she figured that they'd been on Earth, so they must have altered the atmosphere of this place. That starfish thingy she'd helped, it had been breathing oxygen, too. "Hey!" she called. "Hey, can anyone hear me? I'm in a room. Let me out!"

Her voice echoed around the enclosure and soon died away. Taking a tentative step to her left then a few more, she felt around blindly and her hand eventually came into contact with a wall. Hard, metallic and unyielding, it felt cool to the touch and gave her a sense of distance and solidity. With scrabbling fingers, she felt around on the smooth wall, searching for a button. There had to be a light switch around here...

"Hey," she yelled again. Wasn't there supposed to be a captain in charge of this ship — or a pilot or lieutenant or someone? "Can you turn the lights on, please? I need some light!"

Once more, her voice reverberated off the metal walls and died away. She continued to feel her way around the chamber, encountered nothing — nothing but walls — and returning to what she thought had been her original position, took a seat once more, rubbed her bad leg, and wondered where they were taking her.

And why would they take her? With frightening speed, a number of scenarios ran through her mind — none of them good — and each one made her lose it a little more than the last.

One, she was being kidnapped and would become part of an interstellar harem, waiting hand and foot on some fat, turbaned bad guy, but then Karen checked her thoughts at the post. Not only was that a stereotype, she figured that bad guys, and maybe they weren't even human, didn't wear turbans out here.

Two, whoever these people were, they were going to study her, probe her pores and any openings in order to see what made her tick. She'd seen enough flicks on the sci-fi channels to know that aliens always experimented on humans. If they did, maybe they could fix her bad leg while they were at it. Then the thought of being experimented on filled her with fear and led to...

Three, they were going to eat her. When maybe five years old, she'd seen an old television show, something about giant-headed aliens coming to Earth, giving the leaders a big book, and when they deciphered it, they found out that it was a cookbook! Eat hearty... *Pass on that, thanks.*

And why had they come to Earth, anyway? They hadn't come just for her, had they? Was it some kind of expedition in order to capture a specimen and study it? Were they there to conquer the world?

No, they'd taken off, so she could take that idea and stick it comfortably on the shelf. Still, they'd captured her, so what did they want and...

Another tremor of fear ran through her. They'd captured *her. Oh God, let me out of here, let me out.* "Let me out!" she screamed, hammering on the floor with her fists and who cared if it hurt. She had to do something! "Damn it, I'm not a monkey in a cage! Let me out!"

After hammering on the sides of the container until her fists hurt, she slumped to the floor, her voice dying slowly away. "I'm gone," she whispered, and tried to hang on to her sanity. "I'm gone," she repeated over and over, and finally stopped speaking. Then an almost imperceptible shift in the way the container moved told her something.

They were slowing down. Hard to believe, because if you were in space, didn't you travel for a long time? Oh wait, they were aliens. They probably had warp drive engines or whatever they were called that could take you from one galaxy to the next in the blink of an eye.

Karen waited a little longer, tried to get a sense of how fast they were going, and a few seconds later, the ship started to rock ever so gently then with a bump, came to a full stop, which startled her into uttering a brief, "Oh."

"Is anyone out there?"

Right, ask the obvious stupid question. Whoever kidnapped her probably didn't speak English, and she didn't know any foreign languages except a little French. She let out a short humph at her own ignorance. It was a no-brainer that these people weren't from Paris.

With a sliding sound, one panel at the far end of the room opened up and the space filled with light. It was empty, devoid of any machines or computers or consoles. The only thing inside it except for her was the starfish-manta creature in the corner. It was sitting up on three of its legs, blinking at the sudden influx of brightness, and turned its head toward her as she approached it.

"Yawr," it said.

Yawr... It said *yawr?* Maybe it was a greeting or maybe it was the thing's name. "Hi, my name's Karen," she said, carefully enunciating and speaking slowly while pointing to her chest. "I'm Karen. You remember me, right? I helped you on Earth."

The creature merely blinked at her, its purple-gold eyes making an audible clicking sound. It said nothing else, but getting up on two of its tentacle-like legs, it tottered out of the door, swinging one leg in front of the other like a cowboy doing an exaggerated strut. Karen limped after it, wondering exactly where she was.

"Oh...wow," she breathed softly as she faced an enormous landing bay filled with ships that looked exactly like hers. The space the size of three or four airplane hangars — probably more — no less than thirty of these ships sat there, waiting and silent.

Headache forgotten for the moment, she walked over to one ship and peeked inside. It was empty, and so was the next one and the next one. None of them had any markings or numbers or letters. The whole place smelled sterile, and silence ruled. The only forms of life around here seemed to be the starfish-manta and her.

With a sudden popping sound, a round, gray ball materialized in front of her eyes. Startled by its appearance, she took a step back, but it did nothing at first, just hung in the air at eye level. About the size of a grapefruit, it had a large unwinking eye in its center and nothing else. It emitted a squawk and Karen looked at it curiously. "I'm Karen Fox," she said in the same slow and careful manner as she'd used on the little alien. "I'm from Earth."

I also feel like a total idiot talking to a metal grapefruit.

The squawking sound continued then Karen felt something grip her head, but from the inside. It was the ball. It had a hold of her mind!

Try as she might, she couldn't move. This thing had her good and tight, and she stood stock-still as the gray metal ball held her in its embrace. She felt its presence, like fingers prodding and poking her mind. With a sudden rush, the fingers withdrew. Her headache also left and that was something to be grateful for.

"Excuse us," the ball said in perfect English. It spoke with a tinny kind of voice, mechanical and somewhat harsh, but from the timbre it sounded unmistakably male. It also sounded somewhat clipped, as if the person behind it was a university professor delivering a lecture.

"Uh," she started off, not knowing what else to say, "Are you always this polite?"

"We are sorry," the metal ball replied. "It was necessary for us to link with your mind and draw out the necessary data in order to understand your language. We shall not enter your thoughts again."

This thing had said *we*. "Uh, dumb question, but who is *we* and what am I doing here?" Karen mentally kicked herself for asking the most obvious of questions, but in this situation, what else would a person ask?

"This is a collection vessel," the ball said. "We have modified the atmospheric composition so that you will be able to exist. We are known as the Keepmasters."

"You knocked me out," she accused, and her temper flared as she pointed to the ball. "What was up with the laser beam?"

"It was actually a neural stunner, and we apologize for firing upon you. When we arrived on your world, we did not know much about your culture. Our vessel has cloaking devices to hide it from your scanners."

Scanners, Karen considered as her anger faded, if only a little. They were talking about radar. No wonder no one spotted them…

"The files on beings in your galaxy were incomplete," the ball continued. "Our collection vessels are armed with defensive weapons designed to repel possible trespassers and render them unconscious. Initially, the vessel thought you were a threat. We were in error and apologize. We have shut down all the smaller vessels and will only use the mother ship for the rest of the mission until this discrepancy in the programming can be repaired."

Karen let out a snort of derision. This was definitely a shake-my-head moment. Since when could a starship not figure out that someone like her wasn't a threat? Interstellar advanced tech or not, laser beam, neural stunner…oh, who cared? These guys had to be pretty clueless, but too late now to complain.

"So, can I see you guys in person?" she asked. "Or do I have to talk to you through this ball thing? And how can it suddenly pop in and out of here?"

The people in charge made no reply at first then her answer came. "Our world is very far away from your present position. We are relaying the information through the guider, the orb that you see before you. Transmitting our information to you is one of its functions. It also has the ability to send itself, as well as small pieces of matter, from one place to another.

"As for this ship, it is an automated vessel. There are no other speaking beings aboard it, save you. The only means of communicating with us is through our guider. It is also our way of disseminating information to other sentient species."

Karen digested the words and thought about what to say. "So...you're collecting animals?"

"Correct."

"Why?"

The answer came immediately. "A number of years ago, there was a large-scale war among many planets within our galaxy. The war caused great damage to the environments of the worlds."

The guider emitted a green light and a holographic screen sprang up. Karen gasped as she saw a number of images flit across the screen. Bodies, millions of bodies, some human and some indescribable...they were all dead. They lay upon the soil of their planets or in the water, bodies bloated, and blood that was all colors of the rainbow pooled around their corpses.

Abruptly, the images vanished and Karen wiped the sudden burst of sweat from her brow. Her mind reeled at the carnage she'd just seen. "How many..." she began.

"Billions," the guider replied in its unemotional tone. "Countless billions have died. However, we encountered another problem. Once we'd ceased hostilities, we found that many of their rare species were in danger of dying out. We offered to take care of them while they rebuilt their worlds. That is the sole purpose of this vessel.

"Taking care of them is only part of what we do. We must also hide them away so that they may live and thrive and propagate their species once again."

Propagate...what did...? "Do you mean..." Karen asked, suddenly realizing what this metal ball was saying, "Are you saying that this is some kind of zoo?"

After a slight pause, the voice, impersonal and unemotional, intoned, "Correct."

The guider drifted off a few feet in the opposite direction. "Please follow me. We will explain in a way that your mind may understand."

"It will explain in a way so I'll understand," Karen mimicked, but kept her voice low. Talk about condescending. This ball—or the people controlling it or whoever—thought of her as being some kind of dummy. Her mindset shifted when she realized that she was on an alien ship and had zero knowledge of how anything worked, so maybe it was best to shut up and listen.

Trailing behind the floating ball of information, she had a number of questions on her mind, but the ball didn't speak and moved leisurely through the hallway. At the end of the terminal, they approached a wall and it opened magically before her, parting down the middle, and they passed through. She'd entered another curved corridor that seemed to go on forever, and after maybe ten minutes of walking, they reached yet another wall. There, the ball stopped and bobbed in the air.

"What do I do now?" she asked.

A tiny triangle appeared in the center of the wall. "Touch it," the guider said.

Hesitantly, she put her finger out and gently touched the button. A shock ran through her, not unpleasant, and instantly the wall peeled away down the center as the previous wall had done. She faced a cylinder. "Is this your elevator?"

"It is a conveyor tube, yes," the voice told her. "We must ascend to the top of this vessel. There, all will be explained."

Curious, she got in, and the wall closed. The space was circular and only large enough for two people, and it had a hip-high railing attached to the wall. Her finger still had a tingly feeling in it, and she briefly lost her balance as the tube rose fast. In a slight panic, she grabbed on to the railing and clutched it as the elevator took her hither and yon. Within seconds, though, it stopped and the wall peeled away once again. "This is...weird," she gasped. "And what's with the buggy feeling on my finger?"

"Please clarify your statement."

What was it talking about...? *Clarify.* Thinking fast, she said, "When I touched the wall before, it tingled, like you gave me an electric shock or something."

"The feeling you experienced means that you are now attuned to the ship's interior functions," the ball said. "If you wish to go somewhere, you simply press that figure you saw on any wall and the conveyance tube will take you wherever your mind commands it to."

Not sure if she understood correctly, Karen asked, "So...if I think of going to, uh...the cafeteria to get something to eat, this tube will take me there?"

"It will."

Hope rising, she continued with, "What about taking me back to Earth?"

"This vessel is not programmed to do so."

Well, I had to try...

Stepping out of the tube, she heard a sucking sound and turned around just in time to see the wall close up seamlessly, as if the doorway had never been there to begin with. *This is totally weird.*

Another corridor lay ahead, and the ball led the way until they came to yet another wall and triangle. Karen pressed it and when the wall parted, this time she found herself in a room roughly the size of a classroom, filled with screens stationed on the walls. Each of them was roughly six by six inches and there had to be well over a hundred screens, all blank. "What is this place?"

The ball bobbed up and down and a slight humming noise came from it. "Our language is very complicated, but to simplify things, this place is called a Knowledge Repository Center," it finally answered. "The individual characteristics of each species are encoded to each screen. As your mind is now attuned to the inner workings of this ship, you will understand how to access this information."

It hovered silently, and Karen looked at a large metal plaque which sat on the wall above the screens. With a number of cursive symbols on it, it seemed like gibberish at first, but her implanted skills came to life and she read,

We do this for they bring us happiness.
We do this because they have no defense, nowhere else to go and no one to care for them.
We do this in order so that they may teach us what it means to be different and for us to embrace that difference.

"What is that?" Karen asked the guider.

"It is our creed."

"It sounds cheesy." If their motto had come out of the Girl Scouts, it couldn't have sounded lamer to her, but whatever. Someone else had dreamed up the idea.

Turning her attention to one of the screens, she saw it resembled a laptop that had a number of keys with cursive figures on them. Her downloaded skills kicked in again, and she understood which buttons to press.

Choosing 'History', she pressed it and the screen flickered to life.

A tinny voice, not unlike that of the guider, intoned, "The Malurian dragon is native to Maluria in the Delos sector of the Furnal galaxy. Its breeding cycle is once every three years. It exists primarily on fungus from its native world, but can ingest other types of sustenance…"

The screen showed a picture of a creature roughly the size of a rhino that greatly resembled dragons from Earth myths with a sharply pointed nose and elongated mouth, flaring ears, blood-red eyes, and a long, gator-like body covered in scales. The narration continued, saying that the dark navy blue dragon, when threatened, would turn bright yellow and subsequently attack. However, instances of it attacking without due cause were rare. It shunned bright light and preferred to feed at night.

"Ron would love this," she muttered, thinking about how stoked he'd be at finding interstellar life. "Him and his dog…"

"What is this about a dog?"

Surprised that the machine had been listening in, Karen blushed and mumbled something about a friend's pet. "Uh, he had this big animal and well…never mind," she said.

Touching another screen, it showed the creature she'd initially rescued. This was a tolop — it came out as *toe-lop* — found in the moons of Endor, another planet in the farthest quadrant of yet another galaxy. This specimen, the information said, was a baby, barely six months old. The tolop, a gentle creature, dined only on grass and insects. Asexual, it reproduced once a year. It also had no enemies. The computer did not say why.

Maybe it put out some vile smell, like a skunk. If so, she didn't want to find out.

"It looks sort of weak," Karen muttered after scanning all the information, then raised her voice. "And what was it doing outside? Don't you keep your pets in cages?"

"They are not pets, not in the sense that your people think of them," the answer came, and this time the tone sounded somewhat annoyed. "We understand the meaning of the word *dog* and these animals are not in the same category. What is on this vessel? They are specimens, rare specimens, and they are here for their protection. That is all.

"As for the tolop being outside, our former keeper made a mistake and it managed to crawl outside. The tolop is by nature a curious creature. It is also young and likes other beings with a fairly high body temperature. It was not used to the atmosphere of your planet and needed time to adapt," the ball said from over her shoulder.

"Fortunately, you happened by and it was drawn to your ninety-eight point six degree body temperature. In due time, you will learn about the various types of flora and fauna on this ship."

Now what did *in due time* mean? Oh…hang on. The meaning of what the mechanical ball had said hit Karen like a punch to the gut. "Wait a minute. Do you mean…I'm supposed to stay here and…and look after these things?"

"Correct."

And with that, she exploded, smacking one of the screens off the wall. These people had to be crazy! They'd kidnapped her for some kind of Noah's ark-type of deal, and she was supposed to go along with it?

Pissed beyond measure, she swiped at two more screens in a moment of childish rage, and it pleased her to see them clatter to the floor and spin around in a mad dance before stopping. "You kidnapped me and now you want me to help you? You're crazy!"

"There is no alternative," the guider said. "The journey to our destination will not take very long, but the inhabitants of this ship must be cared and provided for. There are no other devices capable of doing what needs to be done."

A snort of disbelief emerged from her mouth. "Can't you get anyone else? I'm, like, sixteen! I'm in high school. I can't walk very well and…" Her voice trailed off. She wanted to tell the Keepmasters about her scars, but pride wouldn't let her.

With a sudden movement, the machine flew close to her and settled an inch away. A blue light emanated from it and she had the feeling that it was scanning her. A second later, the ball confirmed it. "While we are not experts on the human race, from the images and memories we have attained from our brief scan, it seems that you have all the features that your race possesses. You have two eyes, two ears, a nose and a mouth. Your species is bipedal, with organs and skin and—"

"You don't get it, do you?" she erupted. Did these people want her to admit everything? "I…I have a bad leg, I can't walk well, so what more do you want from me? I can't do this. Take me home!"

Rant over, she plopped down and instantly regretted it, as she landed on her tail bone and the deck was hard. Tears welled up in her eyes and she hastily wiped them away. "You don't have any right to kidnap me. You should have left me alone. I don't want to be here."

"There is no choice," the ball repeated. "This ship has been programmed to fly to a number of preset destinations before reaching its home base. There is no possibility to return to your planet, not at this time."

Abruptly, the tone of the machine shifted, became somewhat warmer, and it settled beside Karen's shoulder. "There was another, another keeper. He met with a sudden illness that we could not treat in time."

"What are you talking about?" she sniffled.

The guider floated up. "Go to the far end of the room and press on the wall. You will find your answer there."

Stiffly rising to her feet, Karen did as suggested and went to the wall. After pressing it, it melted away to reveal a transparent sarcophagus in which lay a small humanoid, perhaps four feet in height. She let out a gasp. With purplish-green skin, it resembled a hunchback. Its skull was disproportionately larger than the rest of its body. "This was your keeper?"

The wall closed and the guider bobbed up and down as if pleased. "Correct. His name we never knew, but he served us well and he was a most capable attendant to our inhabitants. Unfortunately, he suddenly became ill and subsequently died. Before his death, he accidentally freed the tolop. That is when you found it…and we found you."

Karen started and shifted her weight to favor her good leg. How long had this ship been in space, anyway? As if reading her mind, it said, "The universe is infinite and the galaxies in which we have traveled are vast. It has taken much time to collect what is needed. We have been in space for more than two of your years. Other vessels of ours have been in space far longer.

"However, our journey is almost at an end. We have only three more species to collect. Their worlds are relatively close to our current position. Once the three have been collected, we shall journey to our home world."

"You still haven't told me where it is," Karen pointed out. Not that she knew anything about what part of the galaxy she was in, anyway, but she figured she had to state her case. "And you still haven't told me what I get out of this. I just want to go home."

In a sudden fit, she stamped her good leg and started to pout. Just as quickly, though, she stopped. Pouting wouldn't help things. The Keepmasters obviously didn't care, and while she didn't want to act like a spoiled child, she couldn't help it. This was so majorly unfair!

A slight humming sound came from the guider. "If you serve us well, if you fulfill your duties, then once we reach our home planet, we will program a ship to send you back to your world. There, you may be reunited with your family and friends."

At the mention of the word 'family' Karen started, and it triggered memories of the bad old days which weren't so long ago. Part of her wanted to say that she had no family and she'd lost all her friends…but pride took over.

Thinking the matter over, she had Ron, but that was about it, and she figured that this guider ball had already searched her memories. "Hey," she began, but an instant later, the little ball disappeared as suddenly as it had appeared the first time, and Karen was alone.

"Crap, I'm stuck here," she said to the wall. This was a prison. There could, and would, be no escape, and she was at the mercy of every living creature on this ship.

Suddenly, the hospital started to look better and better. Her throat constricted as the reality of her situation set in, and she began to cry in earnest. Tears rolled like waterfalls down the sides of her face and she blubbered uncontrollably before drawing in a series of deep breaths. "Stop it," she ground out. "They don't care, so stop acting like a baby."

Crying jag over, she wiped her face off and brushed her hair back as determination set in. She was here and they weren't going to listen to her. At the very least she could say to someone — if she ever got back to Earth, that is — that she'd been in space.

"Right, like anyone's going to be around to hear my side of the story," she said and shook her head at the ridiculousness of it all. Sighing, she got off the floor, picked up the study screens she'd knocked off and started to pore over the data. This was going to take some time, but she seemed to have plenty of that.

* * * *

Time passed and Karen straightened up with a groan. She'd been peering at the screens for…she didn't know how long. It was long enough, though, as all of her muscles locked into place, and they complained when she moved.

Could she do this? There were so many different kinds of life that she didn't know where to start. Maybe it was one thing to take care of a sick dog or cat, but this?

A mistake, she decided. It all had to be some kind of awful mistake. According to the computers, there were twenty different kinds of species living here. During her study time, the ball-guide had popped in to tell her that, indeed, many more ships of this type spanned the galaxy, going about their collecting duties.

"We will repeat that the universe is almost limitless in terms of its reach. Traveling through the various galaxies is very time consuming," the guider said. "Not only in terms of traveling between planets, but also learning about the various species, building the proper enclosures for them, and making sure that our facilities are ready. We do not wish to disappoint those who've entrusted their world's endangered species to us."

A wave of disbelief swept over her. "And you expect me to learn about all of these animals at once? That's nuts!"

No reply came at first and she waited impatiently, tapping her toe and drumming her fingers on one of the screens. Finally, the voice of the Keepmasters came through. "There is time enough for that."

With that semi Yoda-like answer, the guider disappeared and she was alone with the screens. Blowing out a gust of air, she got back to work.

"I gotta do something different," she muttered to no one in particular and stretched out her back and shoulders. She heard her joints crack and pop from the previous lack of movement. It felt pretty decent to just stretch out, and she practiced her flexibility exercises that the rehab specialists at the hospital had taught her, simple toe touches to start with in order to loosen up her hamstrings then she transitioned into harder mobility drills, lunges and squats and other strengthening exercises.

Her leg pained her, and after taking a glance around in order to make sure no one was spying on her, she pulled her pants down in order to examine things. Even with all the rehab she'd done, it was still smaller and weaker than her left leg. With a grunt of vexation, she pulled her pants up and doubled her efforts on the exercises.

Repeating in a forceful voice, "You're going to walk normally again. You're going to do it," she commanded her body to follow through and pushed herself to the limits she'd previously reached — and beyond.

Sweat poured off her body, her muscles ached and her heart rate sped up to a high level, but she kept at it, and finally, body shaking and muscles quivering, she stopped to breathe in and out and concentrated on calming down.

"Good," Karen decided when her breathing returned to normal. "Good effort. Keep it up."

Pep talk over, she wondered if she had any living quarters to go to in order to lie down.

What did the guider say? The ship would respond to her mental commands, and she just had to think of some place to go. "Let's check it out," she murmured and went over to the wall. A triangle appeared as soon as she put her hand on it, and parted under her touch. "Hey, that's not bad!"

Venturing out into the hallway, she moved on over to the wall where the elevator ostensibly was. It opened up under her touch, and she got inside and thought about going to her living quarters. If the former keeper had a place to stay, maybe the Keepmasters had already prepared a place for her, too.

Instantly, the elevator moved downward at high speed then a second later, did a sudden right. The shift knocked her off her feet and she landed on her derrière, uttering a surprised and pained "Ouch!"

The elevator could move laterally. It had never occurred to her that it couldn't. Getting up, she hung on to the side of the tube and three seconds later, the elevator shifted to the left. "Ha, I'm on to you," she declared.

The moment of triumph vanished when the elevator hung another sharp right and threw her against the opposite wall. Banging painfully into it, she let out a, "Crap," and massaged her hip.

"Hey, don't you have a go-slow button here?" she yelled. No one answered, but a second later the elevator began to slow down then it stopped. The door opened, and she found herself facing a blank wall. Where was she?

With a popping sound, the guider appeared. "You are now at the bottom of this vessel," it said. "Your quarters are straight ahead. Touch the wall and enter."

Doing so, the wall parted down the middle. A room lay ahead, but before she entered, she turned to the ball and said, "Do you mind if I call you Guider? Maybe it would be a little friendlier, you know?"

The ball didn't answer right away. It simply hung there, silent and impersonal. Karen wondered if she'd pissed someone off, but suddenly the voice inside the ball said, "You may call the ball Guider. That will be sufficient."

It then vanished, just as it had before.

The room was a small affair. A soft blue color all over, there were walls and the floor and nothing more. It was perhaps twenty by twenty feet square. The floor felt soft and spongy, and she bounced a little with every step. In the far left corner, she saw a few cushions and a blanket. They had blankets in outer space!

Wondering if there was a bathroom and shower, she ventured over to the far wall and put her hand close to it. Instantly, a triangle appeared, and after touching it, the wall parted to reveal a small enclosure, barely five feet in height and perhaps four feet wide. She had to stoop down in order to enter it and realized that she was staying in what must have been the old keeper's room. "Taking a shower isn't going to be easy," she murmured softly.

She touched the wall and it felt like concrete. A number of holes the size of golf balls dotted the walls, and a small opening in the floor with a button beside it faced her. Pressing it, she heard the swirl of water as it flushed and knew she'd found her toilet. Good, so where was the shower?

Turning her attention back to the holes, she saw another button, but didn't bother to press it, as she figured it would turn on the shower. "Ah, I've got you figured out now," she said, unusually satisfied that she'd adapted so quickly.

Well, no, she hadn't—not really. By her count, she'd been in space only about three or four hours plus the time she'd been knocked out. "I'm going to get by," she said. Really, there was no other choice. She didn't know anything about operating the ship. She had no knowledge of where she was going, and there didn't seem to be any way of overriding the computer program. She hadn't even seen a computer outside of the animal information tablets, so strike out the idea of rewiring anything.

"I'm going to get by," she muttered again with grim determination. Playing super-nanny to an intergalactic zoo had never been high on her list of priorities, but what else could she do? The Keepmaster guys said that there were only three more animals to bring in and that wouldn't take so long, so she'd put up with it.

Entering the main bedroom, Karen then examined every square inch of it. She noticed only a couple of panels a few inches off the floor with a single button on top of each, decided not to touch them then yawned, tired from the mental and physical exhaustion.

With little else to think of save sleep, she lay down and pulled the blanket over top of her and positioned one cushion under her bad leg while the other served as a pillow. The room was warm and comfortable and she soon fell asleep under the stars.

Chapter Three
On the job

An alarm went off, startling her from a sound sleep into a state of half-zombie, half-human. The noise was ear-splitting, somewhere between a screaming monkey and an air-raid siren, and why did it have to come now? She'd been dreaming about rocking on an ocean in a comfortable boat, the motion lulling her into a deep state of restfulness. It was all so peaceful, so serene...then some weird beings came along and zapped her with a light beam, taking her captive and...

The alarm went off again, more insistently this time, and the sound knifed through Karen's eardrums and caused her brain to vibrate. "Okay, enough!" she screamed. "I'm up."

Off to her left, Guider hung in the air.

"What was that?" she exclaimed, rubbing her eyes and still not totally aware. "I was trying to sleep."

"It is morning as you would judge it," the metallic voice said. "You have been sleeping for exactly seven hours and twenty-two minutes."

The proclamation startled her out of her semi-dream state and into a state of full alertness. "Oh God, it would have to be real," she said then decided to shut up and get out of bed. Rubbing her eyes and yawning, she felt stiff and sore from the previous day's work-out, but overall, she felt a little more able and got to her feet.

Reality check time came as she looked around. Yes, this was as real as it got. As for it being morning, her internal body clock had adjusted. She'd get by…and a rumble from her stomach told her that she needed to get something in her and soon.

"As is the custom with your people," Guider said, "you must begin the day with food in your body. Find the commissary, and I shall meet you there."

It vanished, and Karen, hungry now, and just as curious as the day before, left the room, found the elevator and thought about the commissary. Immediately, the elevator began to move, obediently sending her on a lateral course to her left. She hung on to the railing and a few seconds later the door opened to reveal a room the size of a convenience store.

No seats or tables…there was only one panel with a button over top of it. Going over to the wall, she muttered, "Can I have my eggs over easy, and do you have bacon?"

Without so much as a heralding sound this time, Guider popped in. "As your mind has now been linked to that of the vessel, think of what you would like to eat, and it shall be prepared for you. The equipment on this vessel now has knowledge of your memories and impressions of what your species enjoys for its meals. It can synthesize any food to your liking."

"Hey, that's a plan!" she responded, and for the first time since coming here, a sense of positivity ran through her.

Turning to the panel, she pressed the button while thinking about bacon and eggs, along with a tall glass of orange juice, trying to make the mental image as strong and as clear as possible.

A second later, the panel slid open and a tray stood there with her order on it. "Whoa, have it your way," she murmured, and carefully taking the tray out, she placed it on the floor, realized that she didn't have any utensils, and mentally asked for them as well. Within seconds, the utensils appeared.

Now armed with a knife and fork, she felt pleased and carefully took a bite. "This…" she said, chewing thoughtfully then with a greater appetite, "tastes pretty decent."

"It is important to have proper nourishment." The response came swiftly, and Karen wondered what kind of people her captors really were. "Although from the brief glimpse into your memory, we do not understand why a fried and fatty food such as bacon is so highly prized among your people."

"Bacon cures just about everything," Karen responded, while stuffing a forkful of food in her mouth. "It's versatile, you can wrap it around almost anything and you can eat it for any meal."

Guider said nothing, and as Karen ate, she wondered what her captors looked like. As she was about to ask, the little ball interrupted her by saying, "When you are finished, please deposit your plate inside the slot. It will be cleaned and put away. Then you will come to the enclosures, and we shall begin."

Once more it vanished, and Karen took her time eating, wondered if she should change clothes then decided that if a slot could prepare food, it might be able to prepare clothes as well.

Since she was already in sweats, she decided to shower up later. If these enclosures were anything like the zoos on Earth, then there'd probably be a lot of poop and pee, so she asked the ship to prepare some rubber boots. They came out a few seconds later, fitting well, and she was ready.

Karen started from the room, and in a sudden trip down memory lane, she recalled her one and only visit to a farm. Her parents had taken her to a local farm when she was younger. The impression she'd had back then — and one which still lingered — was that it smelled and the animals there — cows and sheep and pigs — were incredibly dirty and stinky, and that a cow had kicked her when she'd tried to milk it.

"Why'd it do that?" she'd asked the farmer angrily once she got up, stifling the urge to swear. Her parents were looking on, strained smiles on their faces.

"You were facing the wrong way."

She never went back to the farm again.

While the thought of playing Nancy Nursemaid to a bunch of galactic critters didn't exactly fill her with joy, she really had no choice. What was that old saying? Oh yeah, 'suck it up, buttercup'. She heaved in a deep breath while making her way over to the elevator.

Once inside, she thought about going to the animal enclosure. Sure enough, the elevator whisked her in a sideways direction then downward at high speed. There were no twists or turns, and maybe fifteen seconds later — this ship had to be immense — she arrived at her destination.

"Wow…" Karen managed to get out when the door opened. "This is…some zoo."

It was more than just a simple zoo. It was an artificial park, something easily the size of a football stadium and probably larger, with rolling hills and ponds dotting the landscape. A bright artificial sun shone overhead, illuminating the landscape in a cheerful yellow glow, and the air smelled clean and sweet.

However, this place wasn't all fake countryside, and she didn't see anyone resembling Ma and Pa Farmer. Instead, all she saw were the cages, a lot of them.

No, on second thought, they didn't exactly resemble cages. They were glass enclosures of various sizes. The enclosures were not uniform in size, either. Some appeared to be only a couple of square feet while others were the size of a house. They all held some forms of life that she'd seen on the knowledge screens. Guider reappeared and a slightly larger screen similar in size to an Earth-made iPad hovered next to it.

"This is your schedule," it said. "It contains your duties. They vary on a daily basis, so you must be careful to follow each and every instruction exactly and explicitly. There is no room for deviation."

Having issued the orders, Guider disappeared and the machine dropped into her hands. "Thanks," she muttered.

As she touched the 'On' button, the screen lit up and a number of chores appeared. Clean the enclosures, feed the animals, do not disturb them and so on. "That seems easy enough," Karen said, and walked to the first place on her list, the Malurian dragons. Entering via the touch-door, the lack of light bothered her at first. It was like dusk had settled in. The glow from the alien iPad told her that the Malurian species didn't like light. "Okay, let's see if I can see in the dark."

While not being able to see clearly irked her, what really got to her was the smell. It hit her right away, a stink of wood alcohol and excrement. "God, this is one dirty place," she muttered and breathed through her mouth.

Stepping on something soft, she looked down and saw a hula hoop-sized puddle of what appeared to be gray snot. She shook the sticky gunk off her boot as best she could, but it clung to the material. "This stinks," she said, but continued on.

Slowly her eyes adjusted to the dimness, and she made out the dragon and its mate sitting side by side on a metallic floor dotted with small holes at the back of a large, square enclosure, lazily eyeing her. Two book-sized panels sat near the female.

From her computer, she read that the male was larger than the female and he was, roughly ten feet in length and about five feet high. The female was about half his size, but immensely fat. "God, are these things tame?" she wondered aloud when she noticed that they weren't chained up.

Hang on a second. The old keeper had died from illness and not from injury, so maybe these animals were domesticated — maybe.

As she warily approached them, the female opened her mouth, let out a loud snort, and made a huffing sound. Something arced through the air and landed on Karen's arm. It felt warm and sticky and...did this thing just blow its nose on her? Oh crap, it *was* a nose rocket, just like the one she'd stepped into and...*ick!*

"Thanks so much," she said, mustering up her sarcasm. Slimy to the max, it clung to her hand. No matter how much she tried, she couldn't shake it off. "Don't you guys believe in tissues?" she asked while wiping her hand on her sweatpants. In a moment of sheer helplessness, she turned her head up to the heavens. "Why did it have to be me?"

As was the case with her room, as well as the commissary, the slots had only one button atop each opening, and pressing the first, a mop and bucket appeared, identical to the Earth models. Pushing the second, a hose with a nozzle came out with a small button on top of it.

"And here's our spray gun," she mused. Pressing the button, a jet of what looked to be green liquid came out of the nozzle. It hit the male smack in the face and his head snapped up.

Giving a loud snort, he got up and ambled over to within two feet of her, and a second later another nose rocket landed on her arm. It was probably his way of expressing displeasure. He then turned around and walked back to sit beside his mate. "Again, thanks so much," she said, and began spraying the enclosure.

Odd...when the water hit, it splashed the glass walls and floor then disappeared down the holes. Drainage holes, she figured, but the water seemed to dry instantly, and just as instantly the smell disappeared. She thought of using the liquid on herself, but decided not to. It might be abrasive, and the last thing she needed was another set of scars on her body.

Job done, she wondered what to do next. They had to be fed, but there wasn't any food. "Hey, Keepmasters or Guider ball or whoever's listening," she called out, "what about the eats for the varmints?" Varmints or critters would do, she decided. She really couldn't think of them as animals.

Guider appeared instantly. "I do not understand the comment about *varmints*," it said. "However, look to your right. There is another panel there." It then disappeared.

"Some people just don't appreciate Earth humor," Karen grumped, her mood sour as she walked over to the wall. When she pressed the button, the panel automatically ejected two round objects the size of sandbags. With another snort, the dragon duo got up and ambled over to the sandbags. Sniffing them, their tongues, long and heavy paddle-like structures, shot out and hauled the food in. The sound of masticating jaws began.

"They like it," Karen said and arched her eyebrows in surprise at the whole deal. This was going to be a snap. After returning her work tools to the slots, they closed up and she exited the compound. Surprised and somewhat pleased by her work ethic, she took a deep breath…and inhaled the scent of the Malurian snot. Open air or not, the smell made her dizzy and she held her nose. "Oh, that is just so nasty!"

The computer in her hand beeped. The next job flashed on the screen, and with no time to clean up, she breathed through her mouth and went to visit the tolop. It sat in a small enclosure the same size as her bedroom, and when it saw her, it let out a small bleat and automatically ran over and jumped into her arms. At least the smell didn't bother it, but what annoyed her was that this thing had gotten attached to her in such a short time.

She'd already had enough odors for one day. The tolop nestled in her arms, rubbing its head against her chest.

"Don't get too comfortable," she told the little creature. "You were the one who suckered me into coming here, remember? I'm just doing my job. I don't need to be buddies — don't want it, and don't care."

Naturally, the tolop didn't answer. It just looked at her, large eyes blinking. Then Karen recalled that it liked body heat, so it was probably just looking for somewhere warm to sit, nothing more. "Hey, you like warmth? Why don't you go outside and sit in the sun?" she asked. Oh wait, it wasn't supposed to go outside. Darn...

"Yawr," it answered, and she rubbed its head.

She wasn't prepared, though, for the screech that followed. With a sudden powerful shove of its tentacles, it pushed her away, dropped to the floor and scuttled off into a corner where it continued to screech like a frightened monkey. Disconcerted, she asked, "Now what did I do wrong?"

Consulting her computer, it told her that the tolop liked its stomach rubbed and its head patted. "Ah, okay, okay," Karen said, realizing her faux pas. Slowly making her way over to the creature, she lifted her hands. "Hey, I'm not going to hurt you."

It didn't move and she picked it up and rubbed its belly. The high, piercing sounds immediately stopped. Instead, it made a sound like the mewing of a kitten. "So that's it," she said, understanding now. "I got it."

The place seemed tidy enough. It also had tiny holes on the floor, probably to drain off any waste, but she couldn't see any droppings or puddles. Still, the computer said spray, so finding the slots she took out the equipment and sprayed. As had been the case before, the liquid dried almost instantly.

While she cleaned up, the tolop hung on to her shoulder with a surprisingly powerful grip. "Hey, we're not best buds," she said, mildly annoyed by its clingy nature, but she rubbed its tummy anyway, and it mewled with pleasure, its eyes clicking away like camera shutters at high speed.

Letting out a deep breath, Karen consulted her computer once more, and after putting the tolop down, went to the door. A voice stopped her. "Yawr," the little creature said, and it almost looked sad.

"Yeah, you want another rub?" she asked in a let's-get-this-over-with manner and heaved an exaggerated sigh. "Okay, I'll give you one more, but then I've got to go back to work."

The creature scuttled over and lay on its back. Karen slowly sat down, favoring her bad leg, and rubbed its tummy. It wriggled its legs in a moment of happiness.

Rub-down over, she stiffly got to her feet and walked out without looking back. The sound of the tolop begging for attention followed her, but she had other things on her mind. "This is going to be one long day," she said to no one in particular, but had the feeling all the same that the Keepmasters were listening in her every word.

Breathing in the air, this seemed to be her one moment of freedom. She would have called it a coffee break, but there didn't seem to be an espresso maker around, and she didn't care for coffee, anyway. She was more into tea.

Still, it was nice to relax, if only for a second, and she almost forgot where she was — almost, until she inhaled the smell of the dragon snot. "Gross," she said, and went back to work.

Trekking over hill and dale, her leg pained her at first, but the more she walked, the better she felt. As she passed by one enclosure, she noticed that its sign read *Atmosphere of pure dilurnium – Toxic.* She didn't know what 'dilurnium' was, but the word 'toxic' hit home. So how would she breathe?

Her answer came in the form of a breather that hung on a hook beside the door. To her it looked just like a deep-sea diver's mask with a tube attached to it. She slipped it over her head, and air immediately came through. "Wow," she exclaimed, awed at this simple but vital piece of equipment. "It's just like being underwater...but not."

Guider popped in again to remind her that this was not a sightseeing tour. "There will be time for that later on." A second later, it disappeared.

"Yeah, right, go and do your job," Karen groused and soldiered on.

For the rest of the morning, she received nose rockets and hosed down poop of all colors of the rainbow. This was grunt work, plain and simple. "Why couldn't they have picked someone else...?"

* * * *

Four years ago

"Why couldn't you have picked someone else?"

Twelve-year-old Karen wailed the question to her mother and father as she separated the mound of clothes, toys and books. She then neatly folded the clothes, piled the books, and packaged the toys, and did this in nine separate cardboard boxes, three for each category. It was time for the annual neighborhood charity bazaar, and Karen's mother had volunteered her services. The packaging was almost done. Once finished, Karen was supposed to take the boxes to the local community center where the bazaar would be held.

"You didn't tell me," Karen said, shooting her mother a look that asked the obvious question, that being, why was her mother picking on her.

"I *did* tell you," her mother replied. "I told you on Friday. Now it's Sunday and I'm helping you, aren't I?" She accompanied her statement with a gaze of total innocence.

Emitting a loud groan, reluctantly, Karen went about her task. She'd have rather slept in or listened to music or…anything, but no, she had to do this and waste two hours of precious *me* time. Why had her mother asked her and why now?

"Yeah, you're helping me," said Karen. Her long fingers rapidly folded a shirt and dropped it into the clothes pile. "But you could have asked someone else."

Her mother reached over to stroke her hair. "Dear, there were other people to ask, but if I didn't think you could do it, then I wouldn't have asked. And I'm on the committee. Each year they have someone different package the gifts. The girl who was supposed to have done this got sick, so I said that you'd do it."

Karen listened to her mother's explanation with her sense of outrage growing. There were at least thirty other students who could have helped out, but no — she had to be the one. It was useless to complain. Pouting, she continued her task, hating every minute of it, but the harder she worked, the faster it all seemed to go.

Finally, she put the last of the items in their cardboard boxes and closed the lids. Reaching for the tape, she firmly sealed them shut, and in spite of her losing about two hours' worth of sleep, she felt a sense of accomplishment. "It's done," she said with a sigh, stretching out her shoulders.

"See," her mother added with a smile, "I knew you were up to doing it. Now help me carry these boxes to the car…"

* * * *

The present

Karen snapped back to reality when the handheld device beeped. She still had more chores to do, which consisted of finding out what food they ate and feeding the rest of the animals. While doing so inside the enclosures, she checked on their food supply and kept an eye on the inhabitants, wondering if they were going to stomp her into the ground or give her a new orifice.

In fact, they did neither of those things. A few snorted, most of them spat, but none of them seemed overly threatened by her presence or made any kind of aggressive moves. They did eye her warily, and Karen's scare radar went wild at first, but after a few minutes, she realized that they simply weren't interested.

After finishing up with her last job on the list, she exited the enclosure and took a deep breath. Fine artificial weather or not, by now her leg had started to ache, and after taking a whiff of her body, she muttered, "I reek."

All she wanted to do was to hose down and pass out, but Guider appeared to ruin her off time. "It appears that you have finished with your chores for the day," it said.

"Yeah, I'm done," she said as the fumes hit her hard and her eyes began to water. She attempted to keep the impatience out of her voice, but didn't quite succeed. "Can I take a shower now?"

"You may."

As they moved along the walkway back to the elevator, Guider asked Karen of her first impressions. She saw no reason to lie and said with distaste, "They hate me. They poop or spit or spew on me, and they probably liked the old keeper better."

"Perhaps they did," Guider answered in its unemotional voice. "But you might recall the words on the plaque in the Knowledge Repository Center."

Karen thought about it…something about embracing the difference…figured out they were just animals that wanted to be fed. Fine, she'd feed them, earn her keep and once this job was over, she'd return to Earth and get on with her non-existent life. Still, she'd been thinking about one question the entire morning. "Why are the animals so tame?"

"It is because of a harmless additive to their food," Guider answered. "It contains a mild drug that dulls some of the more volatile specimens' fighting instincts. The faderum, the actillion and the Malurian dragon are all violent in their native habitat, but here, the drug renders them docile."

Karen nodded thoughtfully. The faderum was a large, slug-like thing the size of a Komodo dragon. It crawled on a number of tiny legs and had vicious-looking five-inch-long teeth and beady black eyes. Its mate was identical in size, but had a red coat instead of a black one. The male merely watched as Karen came in to clean up and deliver its food — something that smelled like roasted pork — but it didn't make a move in her direction. The female came over and hissed at her, but abruptly turned away and went back to the corner of the enclosure when the food was served.

The actillions resembled large moths and stood more than fifteen feet in height, had wickedly long tongues, and with lightning speed snatched up the lumps of what seemed to be meat she offered them. In terms of weaponry, their wings had a kind of steel lining that looked frighteningly sharp.

Good thing they're drugged. While she wasn't all that keen on drug therapy — she'd had a lot of painkillers during her stay in the hospital and disliked being on them — in this case, she figured they were necessary and she didn't want to see any of the creatures get pissed off.

In a voice that bordered on supreme impatience, she said, "Okay, if that's all for today, then I'm going to take a shower and get some sleep in."

"You may clean up and eat, but we have another specimen to pick up. We should be landing in roughly three hours."

"Do I have to leave the ship?"

"Correct."

"Why?" she asked, hoping that this machine wouldn't figure her for a hard case. "I mean, don't you have any robots or droids or whatever you call them to handle bringing the animals onboard?"

A humming sound came from Guider. "We do not," it finally said. "We had robotic repair crews at one point, but they met with accidents and are no longer able to function. As for the ship, it is self-repairing for the most part, so there is no need. As well, when receiving the animals from their planets' owners, it is better to have things done face-to-face. It lends a more personal touch."

Karen wondered if the people behind Guider were making a joke. A second later, she decided that they were being earnest. More questions surged through her mind, but Guider vanished and she was on her own again.

After giving a resigned shrug, she went back to her quarters and shucked her clothes along with the boots. Stuffing them into the panel, she padded over to the shower, crouched down and pressed the button. Instantly, the water hit her from both sides like a tidal wave and drenched her, blasting off every bit of crud in less than a millisecond. It had a sweet scent to it, not unlike lilac.

"That was...different," she opined, and once the water stopped, hot air came out of the vents and dried her off in an instant. "And that," she stated, "was pretty cool."

Going into her room over to the panel, she wondered if it would provide clothes. Thinking about it, a second later a one-piece uniform appeared. Orange with black vertical stripes, it seemed wearable and she stepped into it. It didn't have any zippers or buttons, but it clung to her then closed up over her body like some kind of memory cloth. "Oh, this is...also cool."

If it provided clothes, then maybe...*let's do this.* She thought about receiving some playing cards. They appeared instantly, and Karen exulted in playing three games of solitaire and winning them before her eyelids started to droop.

This has been one weird morning. And she passed out.

* * * *

Karen started out of a sound sleep as the monkey alarm woke her. Her heart racing, she asked, "What is it?"

Guider appeared. "We have arrived. I will guide you to the exit of the ship."

With that, the little ball flew out of the room. Karen, still half asleep, yawned and decided that if this was an alien world, she'd probably need more protection for her feet. She asked the ship to conjure up a pair of leather ankle boots, and a second later the boots came out of the slot, a rich brown color, sleek and sexy looking. "Yeah, I'm all about style," she said, and slipped them on.

"Wonder how I look," she murmured, realized that there weren't any mirrors around, and decided not to think about it. The last thing she wanted to see was how ugly her facial scar was.

When she stepped outside, she found that Guider had been waiting for her so she followed it to the elevator. Seconds later, it took them to an open doorway, which revealed a gray planet. "Where are we?" she asked.

"This is Ellasus," it said. "The composition of the air is very similar to your world's atmosphere, so you will not need a breather. We are to wait here for our delivery. The Ellasiuns have informed us that they will come soon. Please wait, and do not wander too far from the ship."

A gangplank had been set up, and she made her way down to the ground, being careful not to trip. Taking in a few shallow breaths to gauge the content, a breeze blew in her face, bringing the smells of smoke, decay, rotting wood and leaves. There was nothing pleasant about this place.

As for the landscape, it was gray all over. A forest stood in front of her, but most of the trees were stunted, showed scorch marks or had been blasted apart, most likely from the previous war the Keepmasters had told her about. Those trees that still stood were roughly the same size and shape as oak trees.

To her left lay ponds full of gray water, and she saw a number of massive holes in the ground, easily the size of a bus and larger. It didn't seem as if anything could still exist on this world, but swiveling her head off to the right, she spotted some flowers. "This is full of drab," she muttered, then turned around to get a good look at the ship.

"Oh wow," she breathed, now fully awake. "This is…"

She wanted to say incredible, but the word wouldn't come out, so she settled for thinking it instead. Easily twenty stories in height, it was round like a ball, roughly the size of two city blocks and probably more. A gleaming black color all over, it took her breath away. Guider popped in. "Is it impressive by your Earth standards?"

Karen didn't want to say so, but this was an amazing moment — something no one on Earth had ever seen before — so she might as well admit it. And she was pretty sure that these aliens knew all about Earth technology. It would seem primitive compared to this. "Yeah…it is," she managed to get out.

"You may touch it, if you wish."

Walking back to the ship and hesitantly touching it, she found it surprisingly warm and pliable. "What is this made of?"

"It is a kind of alloy we produce on our world," Guider said. "It is similar to the platinum and steel alloys that your world produces, but much more flexible and infinitely stronger. Its power source is tranium, an element on our planet, and it can power an object this size, or even larger, for up to a century."

"Uh-huh," she answered, still slightly freaked out by the concept of being on an alien world. Turning around to face the landscape once again, she asked, "What happened here? It looks like a bomb went off."

After a few seconds, the response came. "The war here was more devastating than on other worlds. The people here do not have the same technology that we possess. It has taken them much longer to rebuild their world."

"Oh."

Karen wanted to say more, but a sense of shame washed over her. *I just had to go and shoot off my big mouth.* "I'm sorry."

"It is understandable," Guider stated, and this time its voice held an unexpected note of warmth to it. "Your people are used to peacetime, having enough food to eat and clothes to wear. The Ellasiuns have had to make do with less."

Now the shame and embarrassment dug into her psyche a little deeper. "Sorry," she repeated, feeling like an idiot. Changing the topic, she asked, "Uh, these Ellasiuns, what do they look like?"

"They are similar to the elephants on your world, except smaller. The species they wish us to carry will not require any care, as the specimens are in hibernation. You must simply keep the door to the enclosure locked."

Karen filed away the information and nodded. One of the flowers caught her eye. Roughly the size of a small car and shaped like a tulip with enormous petals, it seemed to move. Flowers didn't move, did they? Oh wait, yes, they did. A word from biology class made its way into her mind—photosynthesis. Still, turning her head to the sky, very little sunlight shone down. "Just a sec," she said, her curiosity overcoming her, and she limped over to the flower.

Nearing it, it seemed to sense her presence and swiveled its head around. "Oh my God, it's…"

Her exclamation got cut off when the petals opened wide, grabbed her around the waist then sucked her in. It was squishy inside, and Karen found herself in a puddle of… She didn't want to think about it.

"Yuck, get me out of here!" she cried and kicked at the side with her good leg. Nothing happened for a moment, so she got up and added some punches to the kicks. A second later, the flower spat her out and shook itself all over, as if ridding itself of her smell or taste. Karen landed hard on her butt, covered in clear gunk, got up slowly, and rubbed the ache away. "What are those things called?"

"Poppers," the answer came. "They are used for the amusement of the natives on this world."

After wiping the slime off, Karen muttered, "Now you tell me," then jerked her head around as she saw movement. Two of the locals were approaching, and she smoothed her hair back, hoping she didn't stink too much.

Elephants were right, Karen thought. With trunks and very large, floppy ears, they stood roughly six feet in height and had bodies shaped like barrels clothed in threadbare dark brown tunics. They shambled over on cylindrically-shaped feet. No toes. The leader nodded at her. She nodded back, and whispered, "I don't speak their language."

"When you bonded with our ship, your mind also bonded with its database center, and that includes our language repository. You will be able to communicate with them," the ball told her.

"And I understood every word you have uttered," the lead Ellasiun said in a gravelly voice. "My name is Tafa. We are grateful for your assistance."

He stared at her, his eyes moving up and down her body. She didn't know whether to be insulted or turned off, yet at the same time it wasn't like he was looking at her as a potential date. Her hand came up automatically to hide the scar, but he continued to gaze at her.

Oh right, give him an answer. "Uh, you're welcome," she said, not knowing how to respond. "Where are your, um…animals?"

"Right here," the second Ellasiun said, his ears flapping in the breeze. He had a sack over his shoulder and opened it to carefully take out two cocooned objects the size and shape of blue watermelons. "These are called matrox. They will hatch in approximately eight months, so you will have time. Please keep them safe."

Karen bobbed her head. "I'll do my best."

Her answer must have not been what the Ellasiun was expecting as his eyes narrowed and his voice came out sharply. "Doing your best is not good enough! Are you not experienced to take care of these treasures?"

Well, hell no, she'd had zero experience, except for one day on the job. And now this guy was lecturing her? What was wrong with this scenario, and what did they expect from her, anyway? "I, uh… I…" Her voice trailed off and she hung her head.

Guider quickly swung over to take up the slack. "Our previous attendant met with an unexpected illness and died. She is our replacement, and she is more than adequate."

The two elephant men turned away, muttering. They seemed dissatisfied and Karen couldn't blame them. She could clean and hose down anything, but taking care of unknown species? All of a sudden she felt the weight of responsibility on her shoulders. At least the Keepmasters had backed her up. Taking in a deep breath, she called out, "Hey, I'm on it."

Both Ellasiuns turned around. "You are what?" one of them asked.

"I mean," she swallowed, "I can handle it. Don't worry."

They glanced at each other, but after a moment, the man holding the cocoons handed them over. "We will trust you."

Karen wanted to say something, but they abruptly turned away and quickly retreated. "Rude dudes," she said.

"More than likely, they are going to make a complaint to us through official channels," she heard Guider say. "Do not concern yourself so. We will make them understand the gravity of the situation."

He *would* have to tell her, though. "Thanks for the vote of confidence," she said. Confidence was something she didn't really have at this point. Heaving in a deep breath, she tried to get rid of the feeling of failure—and couldn't.

As she trekked back to the gangplank while holding carefully onto her precious cargo, she noticed a different kind of footprint a few feet away from the ship. Going over to get a closer look, there were a number of them and they resembled human feet, but they were extremely wide and had seven toes, stubby and square. Maybe it was another kind of animal on this planet.

Back on the ship, she made her way to the enclosure with Guider in the lead. Once there, it pointed out where she should lay the cocoons, a small darkened enclosure the size of a large gym bag. Safely stowed away, the enclosure sealed itself automatically.

"Your duties are now done for the day," Guider said.

It then paused, and when it spoke again, it sounded alarmed. Odd, she thought robots were supposed to be unemotional, but realized that the people behind Guider had to be humanoid or something similar. "What's going on here?"

"Return to your quarters. We must make haste."

"Why?"

It didn't answer. It simply pulled its vanishing act, and Karen figured it had other duties. Back in her quarters, she stripped down and stepped into the shower, but didn't expect the sudden jolt that followed. *Oh, this isn't on the itinerary.* "What's going on?" she yelled.

No one answered her, but another jolt rocked the ship. The shockwave threw her against the wall and her bad leg banged painfully into the hard surface. Karen let out a yelp, but stopped when she felt the ship speed up. Listening carefully, the sound of engines turned on *high* came through to her ears. "We're moving...moving fast," she said in wonder.

Going outside, she got dressed and called for assistance. Once Guider appeared, she asked, "What's going on? Are we, like, at warp factor eight or something?"

"There was an unexpected change in our schedule," the reply came. "We..." Guider hesitated. "We had to depart rather hurriedly and have increased our speed to our next destination."

"It felt like someone was shooting at us," she said. When Guider didn't answer right away, her BS-O-Meter went off. "Well, are you going to tell me?"

"There is nothing to be concerned about," it said and vanished.

"Fine," she muttered, perturbed by what had just happened. She didn't feel any more jolts, so perhaps it had just been the engines firing up. "Whatever... If it's all good, I'm going to crash."

Listening to the sound of the engines, something heavy and powerful, Karen thought about her day. So far, she'd experienced different alien animals, been used as a tissue, been swallowed by a flower and been insulted by some aliens. And Guider had lied to her, she felt. She didn't know why, but something had to be wrong.

Stowing the thought in the back of her mind, she figured that after they went to the next two worlds, her job would be over. In the meantime, there were still two other worlds to go to and more cleaning and feeding chores to do.

"If they're going to wake me up, then I'd better have a clock to tell the time," she muttered. Going over to the slot, she mentally relayed a command for an alarm clock, and one soon appeared. Thinking about it more deeply, she asked for and received a watch, as well as a toothbrush and toothpaste. Now she was ready.

A yawn involuntarily escaped her lips, and after setting set the alarm for seven the next morning, she lay down once more. Seconds before passing out, she wondered once more about what had made those footprints, and decided to ask about it tomorrow.

Chapter Four
Explorations and first warnings

The monkey siren went off loud and shrill the next morning. Turning over on her side, mumbling something about respecting an individual's right to sleep, Karen glanced at her clock. It read six sharp. "Reset time," she mumbled, and set the clock to wake her up at the proper hour. Listening to that alarm scream made her head hurt.

Groaning as she got to her feet, Karen shook out her legs, wandered into the shower, let the spray assault her and came back to put on a fresh uniform and some new boots. Today's style involved choosing a pair of two-inch heeled gleaming black leather boots that went up to her knees. They fit snugly and she felt like a superhero for a few seconds until Guider popped in to announce, "It is time for your breakfast."

It did not mention the previous day's hasty departure, and Karen decided not to ask after all. The ship rocked side to side in a gentle motion, and she had the feeling that they'd slowed down considerably.

While eating a very nice bagel and cream cheese-smoked salmon combo, the daily schedule popped in out of thin air. After turning it on, Karen saw three tasks. Feed the canarians first, then the other animals. Scour the last two empty enclosures for the coming arrivals. Tour the ship. Looking over her shoulder, Guider bobbed in the air, silent and waiting. "That sounds easy enough," she said.

"If you work hard, it shall be."

Okay, enough with the impersonal stuff. "Can you call me Karen, please?" she asked. "You can use my full name if you want. It's Karen Fox, or you can call me Karen. But if we're going to work together or if I'm working for you, then maybe we could go on a first name basis?"

Silence followed, and then, "Very well, we shall use your first name. Please finish up and begin your day."

Of course it was duty time — no pay, just food and a place to live. Hastily stuffing the last of the bagel into her mouth, she then cleaned up and took the lift to the bottom of the ship where she wandered out into the park, schedule computer in hand. After a few minutes, she found the canarians' enclosure. Large and very high, perhaps a hundred feet or more, she expected from the name that they were birds of some sort.

At the entrance, she saw a warning sign — *Breather required.* She took the breather off the hook and fitted it over her face. The oxygen came through automatically and she heard the hiss of her breath. *Feed the birdies. I got this.* "Ready now," she said, and ventured inside.

Brightly lit, it resembled an aviary with a number of green, yellow and purple feathers dotting the floor. A large number of perches lined the walls and hung from the ceiling. Her duties didn't include cleaning up, but the birdies had to be fed, so walking around, she listened for the sound of flapping wings.

A second later, two birds the size of cardinals circled down from overhead and landed on her shoulders. As with many male-female pairings, the male was slightly larger and more brightly colored, and this canarian was no exception. It had a lustrous golden comb on its head covered in red and black splotches. Its body, lean and heavy considering its small size, had the same basic gold plumage, but its wings had a number of green and purple feathers, all of it adding up to a kaleidoscopic whirl of colors.

"You're pretty bright," she observed. In contrast, the female canarian was much duller in color, with muted splotches of green and purple. It then decided to sing out, a shrill, throbbing sound not unlike a hawk descending for the kill. "And you're loud, too."

A peck on her mask startled her. The male's beak, roughly half a foot long, like a toucan's and just as heavy looking, pecked her on the mask again, harder this time. It then opened its mouth and screamed at her in a raucous voice.

"You want breakfast, don't you?" Karen asked, and the female rewarded her question by painfully pecking her head. "Hey, that hurt!"

The duo continued to peck and scream, back and forth, beating a tattoo on either side of her head. *Rat-a-tat, rat-a-tat...* Karen dropped her schedule board and limped over to the wall slot as fast as possible with her passengers still delivering their message.

"Stop pecking me!" she yelled. Their beaks were very hard. Not overly sharp, but hard, and if they broke her mask, she could say goodbye to a very short life.

Nothing was on the wall except a small lever. Desperate to be left alone and slapping at the birds and failing, Karen dove for the lever and yanked it downward. In a flash, a number of seeds the size of her thumbnail poured out onto the floor. "Breakfast," she cried. "Now get off me!"

Immediately, the birds hopped off her shoulders, fluttered their way down to the floor and began busily pecking away. Soon, the seeds were gone, and with a final scream as if to assert their superiority, the canarians flew up to the top of the enclosure and stayed there. Karen stood there, watching blood drip on the floor. She didn't have to check where it came from. The pain told her.

Once she gathered up her schedule-pad, emerged from the enclosure and took off her mask, Guider appeared, and it just had to state the obvious. "You are bleeding."

"Yeah, no kidding," she said. She was still angry and hurt and wondering why life had to be so unfair. "They hate me. The animals hate me, and I'm not cut out to do this."

No answer came her way, so she vented. "You dragged me along on this, gave me no choice…you kidnapped me! I'm doing my best, and all I get is feed me, clean me, do this and do that." She waved her arms in a wild circle and didn't care if the Keepmasters thought her a member of the loony brigade. "They friggin' want me to be their mother. I'm *not* their mother!" she yelled.

On the verge of crying, with rage and frustration, Karen turned and shouted at the enclosure, "How would you like it if I *didn't* give you anything for a couple of days? I bet you'd be more cooperative then!"

Thoroughly pissed off now, she turned her wrath on the ball of knowledge. "Why didn't you tell me they were into attack mode?"

"You did not ask. Please consult your computer."

With a vicious stab of her finger, she switched it on and read the data. *Canarians are known to be voracious eaters...impatient...sedative drugs and other forms of anesthetic, ineffective...must be fed daily and* immediately *upon entrance to facility...*

Wonderful, she thought, Reading Comprehension 101 for the everlasting win. Okay, the canarians had won round one. No wonder they'd been cranky if they'd gone at least a day that she knew of without food. Even so, they wouldn't win again. Her head still hurt, but putting her fingers up to feel around, she found that the bleeding had stopped. Possibility of infection or not, she had to tough it out and decided to get on with things.

While her immediate rage evaporated, her sense of injustice remained. "You could have gotten someone else," she muttered.

"We apologize for taking you, but we—" Guider hesitated, and when it spoke again, its voice had a distinct note of passion in it. "We needed someone to take care of them. You were there."

"I was there," Karen mimicked. "I just had to get nice and stuff a starfish into a spaceship and you kidnapped me."

She silently fumed as Guider continued speaking. "As for the canarians, they were not fed for two days before you arrived and they had no one else to feed them."

A note of sadness replaced the passion in its speech. "It is the same situation with all the animals we carry.

They cannot get the food for themselves, and they have no chance at surviving in the wild on their world or on any other. They have been away from their homes for too long. Even if we reach our own planet and house them in enclosures, they can never return to their home worlds."

Its logic may have been undeniable, but all the same, Karen knew deep down she wasn't good at this. She'd always been afraid of animals and here she was, playing Zooey the Zookeeper. "I'm just not cut out for this," she said, and hated the plaintive note of despair in her voice.

Guider revolved in the air, and it made a low, thrumming noise. When it did speak, it sounded almost philosophical. "There is a tale, a legend among our people. It is said that there once lived a very wise person. He was a farmer, worked hard in his fields and earned just enough in order to live a simple existence. He had no wealth, no fine clothes, and subsisted on the basic food he grew.

"One day he took a walk and found a precious stone in the crevice of a nearby mountain. It was called *finitum*, the rarest stone in existence. He knew that if he could sell it, he would never want for food or drink or clothing again.

"The next day, he met a fellow farmer who had suffered through a severe drought and most of his crops perished. The other farmer saw the stone and wished to have it. The farmer who had found the stone gave it over immediately."

Listening patiently to the story, the last bit puzzled Karen. "Why would he do that?"

"Please wait," Guider said. "I will continue. The farmer who had received the stone knew his life was forever changed by receiving such wealth, but the next day he returned the stone to the one who had found it. He spoke to the first farmer and said, 'this is a beautiful stone, but I shall return it if you give to me something even more valuable'."

Still puzzled, Karen nodded. "Go ahead."

"The first farmer answered, 'It is not what you possess, but that which you have that others need'."

Karen's mouth fell open in disbelief. This was the lesson? What was it supposed to mean? Welcome to BS class and she was the only student. "Fine, that was a tremendous speech," she said, thinking about the five minutes of her life that she'd never get back.

While she wanted to lay the sarcasm on a little thicker, Guider interrupted by saying, "Please go to our infirmary and seek medical help. It is completely automated and will attend to your needs."

"I'm still working, remember?" she said as she checked the list once again. "I don't have time to bleed."

Stomping off, she went about her work and naturally, the animals did what they did best — mainly puke on her, shoot nose rockets and slime and more. After a couple of hours of enduring stinks and stenches beyond human imagination, she couldn't stand her own vile smell.

As she stood on the main path and breathed though her mouth, she wearily consulted her schedule and found that she still had to clean the new enclosures. "Where are they?"

"Please follow me," Guider said, and led the way out.

Trudging up the path, Karen came upon two large glass enclosures side by side. One of them had numerous bars inside, somewhat similar to a jungle gym, while the other one was completely bare. Both of them required cleaning. Guider chose that moment to vanish. Fine, Karen thought, she'd do better on her own, anyway.

Entering the first enclosure, she pulled out a bucket, a large, circular brush with stiff thistles on the end and a hose. This place had to be scrubbed, so she got to work, scouring the floor until it shone, dumping the water all over then hosing it down. Her muscles ached, her still-healing leg had started to hurt all over again, and during her duties, her right arm had decided to go numb.

She sat on the floor, massaging the life back into it for a few minutes. When the feeling returned, she got up and soldiered on. After repeating the procedure with the second enclosure, she looked around for a sign that gave the names of the animals that would inhabit these places. Failing to find one, she checked on her computer and came up with nothing. Sighing, she called out, "Guider."

It appeared in a millisecond. "Yes, Karen, what is it?"

"I, uh, didn't see any signs on these places," she said. "My computer doesn't have any information. What kind of animals are going in here?"

Guider was silent for a time. When it spoke, its voice sounded uncertain. "The first specimen—the one that will enter the enclosure with bars—is from the planet Nar. It is called hebiran, and it is most similar to the snakes on your world. It prefers to sleep on the bars as opposed to the ground, hence the addition of those bars to the enclosure.

"As for the second specimen, we have no knowledge of it. It is actually the second specimen's world that we will encounter first on our schedule, so we must be ready. We will be landing there tomorrow morning."

Excuse me, are they actually admitting ignorance here? "I thought you knew everything about these animals."

Guider's voice retained its uncertainty. "The second specimen is from a world that only recently contacted us. Its name is Plattus, and for some reason, it could not provide us with information."

This whole thing sounds crazy. "So you don't know if this Plattsian or whatever it is could be dangerous?"

The ball bobbed up and down. Apparently, that was its version of nodding. "Correct. And the inhabitants of that world are called Platusians. The name uses only a single t-letter, as your language would spell it."

English lesson given, Karen decided to shower up first then go to the infirmary. Naturally, the infirmary had no one on duty, only a couple of panels, so mentally conjuring up some bandages, two square patches tumbled out and she put them on either side of her head. A cool feeling spread from the sides of her head down to her shoulders, taking the pain away.

A couple of minutes later, she felt around the injured areas and found no blood and no trace of a cut. "Pretty miraculous," she remarked to no one in particular.

Guider reappeared just after she'd walked out of the infirmary. "Will you be resting now?" it asked.

"Yeah, why not," she replied. "I'd like to crash, unless you have something better for me to do."

The pocket guide to the critter-verse appeared in her hands. "There is always something new to learn."

It vanished. Sighing, Karen took the hint and returned to the park. As she walked around, she mentally ran through the food, habits and other trivia about the animals. While making a brief stop at the

Malurian dragons' enclosure, she found the male nosing around. The female was nowhere to be seen.

Curious, Karen entered and the male huffed at her, but this time he didn't shoot out a nose rocket. In the dim light, she saw that the female was lying on her side, breathing heavily and intermittently. The male lumbered over in a flash, but oddly enough didn't do anything more than nudge its mate gently with its nose.

"What's wrong here?" Karen wondered and gently ran her hand over the side of the smaller dragon. It continued to breathe heavily, and its eyes gazed at her, not with pain so much as surprise.

Gently, she continued to feel along the dragon's side until she reached its abdominal area. Like a cow, this dragon had a number of teats, and they seemed to be growing larger. She touched one very gently, and it felt surprisingly soft compared to the rest of her iron-hard body.

A second later, something kicked at her, kicked...as in a limb kicking from inside the female.

"Oh crap," she breathed. It seemed interstellar animal life wasn't all that different from the animal life on Earth in habits and symptoms. She would have given anything to talk with a vet for only five minutes. This couldn't be happening now, could it?

It could. Consulting her guide, she read out the following details on its mating rituals and more importantly, its birth cycles. *Malurian dragons mate infrequently, but for life...give birth once every three years to only one offspring...current female is in the second term of pregnancy...marked by erratic breathing and enlarged teats, soft and malleable...birth imminent...*

Karen stopped reading as an alarm went off in her head. The impossible had happened. This animal was pregnant! She had to tell Guider, but she supposed he must know, but hustled out of the compound as quickly as possible, making her way to the lift. Once inside, she mentally willed it to take her to the main bridge, and a few seconds later, she arrived at her destination.

Stepping out of the elevator, she found herself in a rather small, circular room with a large viewing screen dead ahead and nothing else — not even a chair. No computers, so perhaps they were located elsewhere. "Guider," she called out, and the little ball instantly appeared.

"Yes?"

"The Malurian dragon is pregnant," she announced.

Expecting to be praised, instead Guider sharply rebuked her by saying, "You were told *not* to enter their enclosure unless to feed them. Why did you enter?"

Taken aback, Karen offered a shrug, but her sense of self-righteousness required her to say, "Well, you said that I had to learn about them, so I thought that I was doing the right thing. What's the problem here, anyway?"

"The problem is that we are aware of the female's condition. We did not inform you of the pregnancy as the animal was supposed to have given birth upon landing. The delay in picking up the other specimens was unavoidable, but as a result of that delay, it appears that she will give birth here, on this ship."

"Oh."

Guider continued to lecture her. "The male is very protective of its mate. It could have killed you. Even with the drug we give it, instinct can sometimes override medication."

"Oh…"

Kicking herself mentally for walking into a possibly deadly situation, she fell silent. "I'm sorry," she finally said, suddenly aware of her own mortality. "I'll be careful."

Guider gave her no answer, so instead she turned her attention to the viewing screen. Stars wafted by like pollen on a breeze, and it amazed her that just this sheet of alien metal separated her from the infinite iciness of space. She'd never been into alien tech before, but the plaque had said to embrace the different, so...time to give it a hug. "Uh, Guider, if we're good on the apology thing, can I ask a question?"

"You may," the answer came, and somewhat grudgingly, too. It seemed that the aliens behind this could also experience major mad-ons. "What is your question?"

Cut me some slack. However, she refrained from tossing out a snotty reply. "Actually, I have two questions. The first is...since we're going to Platus," she made a mental note to use a single t-letter then squelched the thought for she doubted that anyone was going to ask her to spell the name for them, "do I need to wear a breather, and the second is what kind of animal life is, uh" — she searched for the word then recalled it from reading the files — "indigenous to Ellasus?"

The reply came instantaneously. "To answer the first question...no, the world of Platus has an oxygen-nitrogen atmosphere and is located roughly the same distance from its sun as your world is located from yours. That is the extent of our information.

"As for the second question, consult your handheld device."

She took it out and searched, but found nothing. "There's no information here," she complained. "What I saw were like footprints."

"Footprints," Guider echoed. "Please describe them."

How to describe something alien? "Uh, well, they were pretty wide, like a quadruple E-size shoe on my world, and had seven toes." She thought a little more, and recalled the depth of the footprint. Putting the facts together, she added, "It was sunk in pretty deep, sort of like the creature was heavy. Does that make sense?"

No answer came her way, so she waited, tapping her good foot impatiently. When Guider finally answered, its voice actually held a note of fear. "If that footprint's description is true, then whatever made it is not native to that world."

Not native... Her mind worked overtime. "So...you mean that other people went to that planet?"

"That is the most likely possibility."

Guider fell silent once more, only to start buzzing a few seconds later. "We are going to enter the atmosphere of Platus very soon. Please be seated, Karen. The entry is always somewhat rough."

It hadn't been before, but maybe that was due to her being in a different part of the ship and also being asleep at the time. Carefully taking a seat, she watched as a planet, black all over, swam into view, and she felt the ship shudder. "Beginning descent," Guider said. "We are engaging the heat shields. Do not be alarmed."

At first she wasn't, but when the speed increased and the flames caused by friction began to appear, then it was time to freak. The shuddering got worse and that almost made her lose it downstairs. "Does...does this ship always do this?" she asked, trying not to sound too scared.

"Yes."

The one-word answer did not comfort her in the least, and although she tried to suck it up, the sweating started and continued until the flames died away. The ship slowed quickly then landed. When it did, it was not with a jarring impact but a slight thud.

"We have landed," Guider informed her.

Karen breathed a sigh of relief. "I'll go to the entrance," she said without waiting for an answer.

Once she'd arrived, the little ball approached her, and it sounded almost regretful. "It seems that we have made an error," it said. "We are here to pick up a specimen. This is not what was expected."

Not fully understanding, she asked, "Why? Is it dangerous?"

"See for yourself."

The door parted, and Karen let out a gasp. The entire area had been utterly destroyed, with the remains of shattered buildings, rocks, glass, rubble and wood strewn around. While the smells on Ellasus could in no way have been compared to a rose garden, here the stench was overwhelming. It reminded her of roadkill at high noon, and it seemed to worm its way into her nostrils and sink into the pores of her skin.

As she scanned the horizon, she wondered where the people were. Even if some of them had died, she expected to find bodies, but nothing moved save one figure that trotted over to the ship.

It warily approached, but on two legs, not four. Finally, Karen's eyes made out a small humanoid with a large skull and enormous brown eyes. It stopped five feet away, a hopeful look on its face. It wore a long, shapeless, light blue tunic and no shoes. With a swirling shock of brown hair, a tiny nose and a wide, generous mouth, it resembled a monkey, but looked far more human.

"Hi," Karen called out. "Can you understand me?"

The person abruptly halted and made a series of raspy sounds while gesticulating with its hands. Guider floated over and bathed her face in a blue light then flew back to Karen's side. The person then spoke in a young girl's voice. "My name is Ralus," she said. "I'm the specimen."

For a second, Karen stood stock-still, wondering whether she should be grateful that she had someone sort of human to talk to or whether she should be afraid. Caught by indecision, she looked at the girl, then at Guider, then back to the girl. Before she could say anything, though, Guider took over.

"We seem to have some miscommunication," it said to Ralus. "We were told by your planet's leaders that there was an animal specimen to be picked up."

"I sent that message," the young girl replied in a trembling voice. "Everybody's dead. There's no one else."

From the way she spoke, this girl sounded like she was around twelve. *But with aliens, who knows how old they are, anyway?* That was Karen's first thought, but then she realized that if anyone was an alien here, it was she. Every creature on board this ship was also alien, so what did it matter? With a sudden change of heart, she piped up with, "Uh, Guider, if she's telling the truth, then why can't we take her along?"

The voice, when it answered, sounded severe. "In their first and only transmission, the leaders of this world informed us that there was one remaining specimen —"

"And I'm that specimen," Ralus interrupted in a voice filled with passion as well as pain, her eyes welling up with tears. "I contacted you. My parents are dead. Everyone I know is dead, and so are all of the animals. If you have something on your ship that can find anyone here, then tell me."

Her lower lip began to quiver and she knuckled away a few tears with a dirty hand. Guider did not respond at first, but then it made a series of clicking sounds. A minute later, it confirmed Ralus' statement. "It is true. There is no other life here."

Karen's mouth fell open. *What could have happened?* As if reading her mind, Ralus pointed at the burned out ruins of what had once been her world. "They came. They came and killed everyone."

"Who came?"

"The poachers did."

"Poachers," Karen started to say and stopped as an awful thought came through. "Did, uh…you get a good look at them?" she asked the girl.

Ralus nodded. "When they first came, they were in a ship and called our people," she said, biting her lip. "They told us to give up our animals and resources. When our leaders said no, their leader — he said his name was Blaron — shot at us from the sky. It was a kind of white light and everything got blown up."

Her body began to shake, and she turned and swept her arm around to indicate the devastation. "This is what happened. Then their ship came to this planet. Their leader is a big man with large feet."

Bending down, she drew a picture in the dirt with her finger. It looked like a cross between a super-heavyweight weightlifter with enormous legs and gut, and a pig, as the face was extremely round and porcine looking.

What came through more than anything was how the girl drew the foot. It had seven toes, exactly like the footprint Karen had seen on Ellasus, and a shudder of fear ran through her. If these poachers could do what this girl said, then this was something she couldn't handle and didn't want to.

And why hadn't anyone *told* her there were poachers around? This kind of misinformation deal meant that she'd have to have a talk with Guider and it would be soon. Swiveling her head around, she addressed the floating ball. "Can't we take her?" she asked.

"It is not possible," Guider answered.

This is total BS. "If she's the last person around, then we have to help her," Karen insisted. This situation sucked and in the worst way, with all kinds of danger coming from every corner of space, and she was right in the center of it. "We're all species, aren't we?"

Guider remained silent and she pressed her point. "If we're all related to animals or if we came from animals or something, then we have to take her. When those poacher guys come back, you know what they're going to do to her."

"Very well," the answer came. "We will take her."

Quickly gesturing with her arm, Karen ushered Ralus on board. "Hurry up," she commanded, "we're going to take off soon."

As the door closed, she heard the sound of engines being fired up and felt the ship shudder. Karen grabbed her arm and pushed her toward the door that led to the lift. "You're coming with me. Guider!" she yelled.

It appeared immediately. "Yes, what is it?"

"I don't know much about spaceships, but I know we have to get out of here. So take us to Nar and let's get this over with. Ralus and I are going to the bridge."

"We are headed to Nar at this moment."

Guider disappeared, and Karen took her humanoid cargo up to the main bridge. Once there, Ralus walked to the screen and put her hand on it, her eyes filled with wonder and awe. "I have never seen anything like this. Our planet…we don't have ships that can travel in space."

She then turned around. "What is your name?"

Karen nodded, trying to be friendly. "It's Karen," she said. "Doesn't… I mean, didn't your planet have any kind of weapons?"

Ralus shook her head and her voice, when she spoke, sounded utterly haunted. "We didn't. We're farmers — most of us, anyway. My father was a farmer. My mother stayed at home with my younger sister and helped my father with the crops. They were killed in the first attack. I ran and hid. When the bad men came to the planet, they shot everything and everyone."

In a low and dead monotone, she recounted the slaughter. "They kept shouting at people to show them their riches." Her voice began to tremble and she seemed on the verge of crying. "We didn't have any. Finally, all the shouting stopped. I came out of my hiding place, found a radio and called for help. The people said they'd help me."

Curious now to see if she knew anything about the people who controlled this ship, Karen asked, "Did you get a name?"

"What?"

Defuse the situation. This girl had to calm down. "First off, take a deep breath. I'm listening."

Ralus did as instructed, but she'd begun to cry now and tears coursed down her face. "I'll... I'll try to relax."

"Good. Did they — I mean the people you called — did they tell you their names?"

Ralus wiped her eyes with a shaky hand. "No, they didn't. There was a lot of noise on the radio. I only had enough time to give them my message. After that, the radio didn't work anymore."

Abruptly her voice cut out and she sat down to stare at the screen. Neither of them spoke, but then Ralus pointed with her finger at a fast-moving dot. "What is that?"

Karen squinted and thought that she saw a ship in the distance. "It's probably them. Guider!" she yelled.

The guide-ball appeared instantly. "Yes, what is it?"

She pointed at the screen. "Is that what I think it is?"

A humming sound came from Guider. "I will magnify the image."

Instantly, a larger picture emerged of what had to be the poachers' ship. Long and shaped like a cone, it had what appeared to be cannons mounted on the top of its hull and along its sides, and Karen did not want to see what they could do. Guider provided the commentary. "Scans indicate that the ship is of alien origin and is headed toward Nar."

It then became clear to Karen. Those dudes had been the ones shooting at them yesterday. That's why they'd taken off so fast. In order to make sure, she asked, "It's the poachers' ship, isn't it?"

"Correct."

"They were the guys who shot at us yesterday?"

"Correct."

At that, she blew a blood vessel. "Oh great, first you kidnap me and *now* you tell me there are poachers out there waiting to kill me—er…us," she added, as she took in Ralus' shocked gaze. "Why didn't you say anything before?"

"You did not ask."

"Crap!"

With that, heedless of her bad leg, she got up and moved over to the lift. With a sharp gesture that cut the air, she waved Ralus over and the younger girl obediently followed the command. "She needs her own room," Karen announced, pointing at Ralus. "She is not going to stay in an enclosure. Specimen or not, she's a person. Is there another room?"

"No, there is not."

On a ship this size, Karen highly doubted it, but asked anyway. "Why isn't there one?"

In answer, Guider emitted a yellow light and what looked to be a floor plan of the ship sprang up and unfolded in the air. It showed more than thirty levels, each with a number of sub-compartments, but looking more closely, many of them were dark. "Essentially, the ship itself is one large containment area," it said. "You were told before that there were once robotic devices aboard, were you not?"

"Yes."

"On a previous mission, we encountered the poachers and they fired upon us. The attack destroyed our robotic helpers. As well, there was significant damage to some parts of the ship. While this vessel is capable of self-repair in most cases, the damage was too great and it was necessary to close off certain portions that were of no use. Those are the dark areas you see. It was also necessary to reallocate resources in order to—"

"I get the message," Karen interrupted, waving her hands impatiently. "Fine, so we can share the room you gave to me." This kind of bureaucratic red tape was frustrating to the max. Couldn't the keepers of this zoo figure out that Ralus was a person and not a lab rat?

"Come on," she said to the girl, took her by the hand and they went to her quarters. Ralus seemed awed just getting into the elevator. Once they reached Karen's room, she stood at the entrance, hands to her mouth, and swiveled her head left and right.

"This is your home?" she asked.

"It is for now. It's yours, too."

For the first time since they'd met, Ralus smiled. "I've never had a room this big. Our farmhouse was small." She took a few steps inside and twirled around on the floor, her smile growing broader.

Since she seemed to be adjusting, Karen decided to go back to the bridge. "Listen, you're going to stay here. I have to go. Got it?"

"I'll be fine."

Karen took off and went back to the bridge. Summoning Guider, she asked, "How far is it to Nar?"

"It will take approximately thirty-six hours at top speed," Guider answered. "We have outrun the poachers for the moment. In that time, you must still perform your duties. If you have any free time, I shall tell you more about the poachers, if you wish."

"How about you tell me now?" Karen countered. She remembered that a tour of the ship was on the menu, but that could wait. This was important.

The little ball bobbed up and down. "We shall tell you."

Chapter Five
History lesson

The main viewing screen showed the vast tableau of inky space, dotted with bright lights that rushed by. For anyone else, it would have been a dream. Take off to the great unknown, seek out new life forms, communicate, have adventures and more, but this was no dream and Karen didn't want to be here. Now that she'd heard about the poachers coming in and wasting everyone, she *really* didn't want to be here.

Still, the whole idea of being in space was awesome enough for her to give the stars her attention until the idea of poachers took priority. Guider hung in the air, rotating to the left then to the right as if waiting for a command. Karen gave it. "So, start talking," she said.

In answer, a green light emanated from the ball and a hologram of the galaxy sprang up. She stared at the image in wonder. It was so vast that it took her breath away. There had to be hundreds of planets, but looking more closely, most of them had halos around them.

"This is the quadrant of space that we are in now," Guider informed her. "This used to be one of the most densely populated areas of the galaxy, with over five hundred worlds, but only fifty habitable ones. At least, there were. The rings of light around the worlds indicate that those worlds no longer contain any form of life."

"No life?" she asked, shocked.

"No life."

Guider's reply stunned her into silence. How could these people murder an entire planet? This was totally crazy! After digesting the news report, Karen's mind turned over and she asked, "So what happened?"

The projection shut off. "In our history and perhaps yours as well, there are individuals from other galaxies that are raiders. They seek to steal riches, resources and other precious works of art or technology from different worlds. In the past, we fought against them and defeated them, but then we had our own wars and our own concerns. The raiders rose once more and became poachers. They have clients from different galaxies who wish to keep various animals."

"Why? As pets?" Karen wondered.

The ball bobbed up and down. "In some cases, yes, they seek these animals as pets, as they serve as status symbols of sorts. These individuals who desire them are wealthy and will pay any price."

"So who is this Blaron guy?" she asked. "Ralus told me his name. Do you have any data on him?"

Guider whirled and made a number of clicking sounds before answering. "This data is unknown to us. There have been numerous poachers from all over the galaxy, and they do not associate with one another.

They are rivals, and they often kill each other in their efforts to secure specimens."

It all sounded like how the poachers on Earth acted. "That's all?" Karen asked. "I mean, they just want the animals and sell them, right?"

"Not quite all," Guider said. "They also exploit the animals in various ways, such as taking their offspring or using secretions from their skin. The Malurian dragon secretes a certain liquid during the second stage of its pregnancy. That is then synthesized into a narcotic which is sold on the black market in some parts of this galaxy and others.

"As for the Ovillian sandworms — which are on another ship — they lay eggs, and while the species is not worth much on the black market, its eggshells are considered a delicacy on certain worlds. There is always a market and someone who will pay. The poachers fill that need."

As Guider spoke, Karen got more and more pissed off. They hadn't told her about this. They'd kidnapped her to play nanny to some smelly animals, and *now* they decided to inform her that, hey, angry beings with big feet wanted to steal the animals and maybe do a number on her just for kicks? "Crap," she muttered. "This whole thing stinks."

"The galaxy is vast," Guider said after a time. "We were of the hope that we would be able to collect the necessary species before they found our position. We were in error."

Karen thought about what she'd just heard. "Then if they're so strong, why don't they attack your world?"

A note of triumph — or perhaps arrogance, she couldn't decide which — entered Guider's voice. "Our world is very well protected. We have a vast global planetary response system, something like the orbital space stations your people use, only they are much more powerful. We have never been defeated."

It all made sense, but Karen still wasn't convinced. "So…they can't get at your planet, but they can get at the ships?"

"Correct. They have already attacked two of our vessels. The ships were automated, so no life was lost, and we managed to eject the enclosures once the ships were within range of our world."

"Eject?"

Guider rose into the air. "Come with me to the engineering section. I will explain."

It vanished, and after Karen got into the lift, she conjured up the image of zooming to that section. Thoughts of Star Trek and dilithium crystals circulated through her mind. "Beam me up, Scotty," she murmured. Her murmur segued into a yelp as the elevator plunged straight down then hung a sharp right in a zigzag fashion until it finally came to a stop.

During the ride, Karen hung on to the railing for dear life, but once she stepped out of the lift into a room not much larger than the commissary, a sense of disillusionment overwhelmed her.

A number of metallic boxes, roughly the size of large-screen television sets, lined each wall. Rubber-like conduits ran from them through another wall, and only one control panel the size of a small bookcase stood directly in front of her with the lettering 'Injection Vent' written on it. A fist-size opening was in the center of the Injection Vent bookcase, and that was all. Karen blew out a deep breath. "This is it?"

"You are disappointed?" Guider asked.

"Well, yeah. I mean, this is a big ship, so I thought the engines would be huge or something."

"Size does not matter to our people. It is what the engines can *do*. And our engines are quite capable of propelling our ship at a reasonably rapid speed."

Guider went on to explain that in the event of a catastrophe, the enclosure pods served as mini-arks, ejected if within range of a habitable planet. "They are all automatically controlled through us — that is to say, our Guider. It is a last resort, but it is something that we have built into the ship should it become necessary."

Karen wondered if there was an escape pod for her, but then decided to file that question away for another time. She believed that this ship would get to wherever it was going and that she'd be going home soon. After all, there was only one more species to get, and once that was over, say hello to her pit stop then back to Earth.

The tour continued. In short order they visited the incinerator where all the waste from the animals went. "It is kept here," Guider said, and it hovered over an enormous vat.

Fumes emanated from it and Karen almost gagged. "It stinks!"

"Unfortunately the waste byproducts from the animals contain a great degree of ammonia and other substances that your species would consider noxious," Guider replied. "However, when burned, they are converted through a process to provide oxygen for you as well as an appropriate kind of atmosphere for those animals that do not breathe oxygen."

"It's a good trade-off," Karen decided, holding her nose. "Let's get out of here. I have to breathe real oxygen somewhere else."

Guider then ushered her to another part of the ship where a small storage room held a number of mops, buckets, tubing and hoses. In yet another room, Karen found some books and scrolls of parchment written in an unknown language. She couldn't decipher them and asked what they meant.

"They belonged to the previous keeper," it replied. "He did not wish to throw them away, yet he did not keep them in his room. He did not tell us why."

"Couldn't you link with his mind or anything?"

Guider swiveled left and right in the simulation of a person shaking their head. "We tried, but his mind was locked off from any contact. Apparently, it was a trait shared by all his people. There was no way to enter hence we never knew his name. We only know that he served us in a most capable fashion."

"Uh-huh," she said. There didn't seem to be too much to say about him. He was gone and wouldn't be coming back.

Since Karen had to wait, she asked if she could go to the Knowledge Repository Center. "Why do you wish to go?" Guider asked.

It was a big ship. She had a lot to learn, and she didn't feel like getting pooed or peed on by the interstellar menagerie. "Well, I'm here for now," Karen replied, feeling that she had to do something in order to keep busy. This news of the poachers killing a planet had upset her and she wondered how bad Ralus had to be feeling. To mask her emotions, she answered, "It'll give me something to do. And Ralus needs to grab some sleep, too."

"Very well," Guider answered, and vanished.

In school, Karen excelled at English and did well at chemistry and math, but this was a different kind of study altogether. Feeling that she had to learn, she buckled down and got to it, checking on everything necessary. After two hours, her mind shut down and she wandered back to her room. There, she found Ralus asleep in her bed of cushions, the blanket over top of her.

At least she could sleep peacefully. She was away from her past horrors. What other horrors lay ahead, Karen wondered, and summoned up another blanket along with three cushions.

She lay down and after propping her bad leg under one of the cushions, tiredness overcame her, but before passing out, a tentacle tapped her on the head. The tolop stood there, a mournful expression on its little face. "Yawr," it said, and she groaned.

"Fine, c'mere," she commanded. She gave it a rub on its belly and it let out a satisfied mew and flopped down beside her. "Good," she yawned. "I need a nap after all this."

* * * *

"Karen, wake up!"

Startled, Karen sat up quickly, blinked, and found Ralus looking at her with a mournful expression. "What is it?"

"I'm hungry."

Rubbing her eyes, Karen crawled over to the panel. "Did Guider, uh, the metal ball, link you to this ship?"

"No."

This was just one more bit of good news which did not make Karen's day. "Guider," she called out, and the little orb promptly appeared, "can't you link Ralus' mind to the ship?"

"Initially we did," it answered. "However, the attack by the poachers damaged some of our systems. The mind-link communication system was one of the systems damaged. She hadn't been linked long enough for it to remember her, as it does you. The only part of the link that still works is her language. Should she need assistance, then it is our hope that you will be able to help her. She is still, after all, a child by your standards."

Karen almost experienced a mini-hemorrhage when she heard this. Part of her felt sorry for the younger girl, but the rest of her remembered that she had a job to do and she sputtered out, "So I get to play Mommy *and* take care of the animals, too?" She smacked the panel in a sudden rage. "Tell me something else."

"As you have noted, Karen, our trip to Nar then back to our world should not take very long, assuming the poachers do not interfere once again. We ask this of you."

It disappeared, and Karen's first instinct was to tell the ship to go shove its engines somewhere dark, small and painful, but she shut her mouth when she saw the moist look in the younger girl's eyes. A sense of shame swept over her. Acting all snotty wasn't on the menu. Swiping her hair back, she asked, "Do you have some special diet?"

"We can eat anything," Ralus quickly replied.

When in doubt, go with the basics. Karen mentally ordered a large plate of bacon and eggs. "This is Earth food. There's more where that came from, so eat up."

Once the plate of food arrived, Ralus used her hands and scooped up the food, shoveling it into her mouth at a frightening rate. Bits of egg clung to the sides of her mouth, and after she belched, she looked up with a guilty expression on her face. "I'm sorry. I haven't eaten for a long time."

This had to be on the high side of bad manners, but Karen realized that customs had to be different wherever one went. She had to get used to that difference. "Well, don't worry about it. You were hungry, right?"

Ralus offered a solemn nod. "It's good to eat with a friend."

Those seven words, simply spoken, made Karen inwardly beam. "Yeah, it's pretty cool."

* * * *

Later on, they took a walk around the ship, and the younger girl pestered her with questions about life on other worlds. "I don't know anywhere else," Karen replied, suddenly weary. Eating lunch with Ralus was fine, but being asked everything under the sun and stars could make someone very tired, very fast. "I only got here the other day."

"Can you tell me about your world? I'd like to know." Ralus' voice sounded eager.

Anything to pass the time, Karen thought, and proceeded to relay as much information as she could. At the end of thirty minutes of basic Earth history, Ralus exclaimed, "I never knew other worlds like yours existed! You talk of flying machines and moving pictures on screens of plastic material. I want to see it!"

Karen offered a smile. "Maybe you will, someday."

Privately, though, she thought that Ralus would be better off somewhere else. She'd have a hard time fitting in on Earth...

Then Karen checked her thoughts. Her own life on Earth hadn't been much fun since the accident. At the very least, the other girl hadn't mentioned the scars, so there was that to consider…

Without so much as a warning by Guider, the alarm went off, and Karen yelled, "What's going on?"

Guider popped in. "We are under attack," it announced. "Please come to the main bridge."

It disappeared and immediately Ralus' good mood vanished. She whimpered, "The bad men are here," and sank to her knees, hugging herself.

This was no time to act like a baby. Karen pulled Ralus to her feet and took her over to the elevator. While she didn't have to utter the order, she felt like it, as someone had to take command. "Bridge," she said, and the elevator started to move.

Once on the main bridge, Karen saw that the screen indicated the poacher's vessel hung off the starboard bow. Pulses of light came from their cannons. Seconds later, Karen felt the impact and the ship rocked back and forth. Ralus started to shiver, but didn't cry out.

"Guider," Karen called, and it appeared in front of her. "Can't we outrun them or something? We did that before, right?"

"We are formulating an idea."

While they're trying to figure out things, we'll probably get blown up. Then a beeping sound came from the screen. "What's that?" she asked.

"They are hailing us." It flew closer, to hover over a green button on the wall next to the viewing screen. "Press that," it instructed.

Doing so, a second later, the image of a very large, extremely fat pig-faced humanoid wearing a filthy white pullover filled the screen, and Karen involuntarily took a step back. Ralus was a good artist. Her drawing in the dirt had given an impression that these people were scum, and Karen was not disappointed.

The figure on-screen seemed to be in his forties with dark, filthy-looking hair that hung down to his shoulders and a permanent sneer nailed to his pale and pink-skinned face. It seemed that bad guys always had to sneer. Perhaps they had nothing better to do. Maybe they thought they'd be tougher this way. When he spoke, menace dripped from his every word.

"My name is Blaron. I am the leader of my crew," he said and his voice sounded like a toilet flushing. "Where we are from is not important. Where you are from is not important, either. What is important is that you are to surrender your stock to me immediately."

Hell no on that. Not that she was into animals, but this pig had fired on them and killed a planet! "I'm the captain," she said, lying through her teeth. "Back off."

Her answer caused Blaron to double over with laughter. "Girl, you are no more than a child! You are no captain. You must be a stowaway, and behind you I see a Platusian, cowering, as all their people cower."

His laughter abruptly stopped and the meanness shone through. "Pardon my poor use of language. There *are* no more Platusians to cower. If you do not wish to suffer the same fate, I will give you a chance and one chance only. Surrender your cargo, and I may let you live."

That chance was no chance at all. "Try it and you'll be sorry," Karen answered, and then realized what a stupid response that was. This ship had no significant weapons and the distance between them wasn't enough. There was no way they'd be able to outrun an attack vessel.

Guider swung down to whisper into her ear, "We are approaching an ice belt."

The image on the main screen shifted to show a field of white rocks that seemed to stretch across all of space itself. They lit up the darkness like glowing ice crystals. "That's ice?" Karen whispered back.

"It is. It is an immense belt which lies halfway between here and Nar. It will shield us if we can enter it."

"Uh, yeah," Karen replied, wondering if there was another way out of this. "We don't, um…have any other options?"

"Surrender is not an option. Poachers never take hostages."

A quick decision had to be made. If one had to hide…

"Let's hide there," Karen ordered *sotto voce*.

The ship moved to its left, and as it did so, Karen got a very bad feeling as she studied the fast approaching rocks. They were gigantic, the smallest being the size of a barge, the largest being something on the scale of a square city block. Her knees began knocking together and she fought to keep her features composed. It wouldn't do to show fear.

The picture shifted back to Blaron, and a look of alarm had also appeared on his face. It seemed that he wasn't too hot on the idea of entering the ice field, either, and his image faded, replaced by the image of approaching rocks.

With excruciating slowness, they made their way into the ice field. The ship shuddered a few times from the impact of hitting the ice. Ralus moaned softly, but said nothing. Seconds later, the ship stopped. "Our shields are up and we are hidden," Guider said.

Karen had no idea if the poachers were following or waiting outside, so she asked the obvious question. Guider hummed and recited, "The rocks here emit a magnetic field which interferes with any attempt to find us by sensors. They cannot enter for their ship is not strong enough to withstand the impact of the ice. This vessel is."

"Then we're safe for now," Karen said, but then she realized that they'd eventually have to come out of the ice field in order to land on Nar. What would they do then?

Guider interrupted her thoughts by humming again. "This vessel has been damaged. Multiple systems are offline. Our engines have also suffered damage. Repairs will be made and all life support systems will be left functioning. Karen, please make sure of the animals wellbeing."

Her schedule iPad appeared before her and dropped into her hands. Danger or not, she had a job to do. "I'll take care of it," she said.

Going to her quarters, Ralus tagged along silently. Once there, she turned to Karen with an apologetic look on her face. "I'm sorry for not doing anything to help you before," she said. Her body still trembled and her voice shook. "I was scared."

"I was scared, too."

Actually, Karen was surprised she'd talked back to that poacher pig. He was nothing but a murderer, and while she'd felt badly for Ralus before, now she felt supremely sorry for her. Having to do a nanny's duties didn't make her day, but there was no one else who could do it and Ralus needed help.

Putting her hand on the younger girl's shoulder, she pitched her voice low and tried to sound confident. She had the edge in years and in maturity, so it was time to suck it up and move the troops out. "Listen, it's normal to be scared. It's normal, but you heard what Guider said. We have a job to do, and I'm going to need your help, okay?"

Ralus gave a hesitant nod. "I think I can help you. I sometimes worked in the fields, carrying in the fruit and berries my mother collected. I'm a lot stronger than I look. I *can* help you."

Karen forced out a smile. "Then you're hired."

"What does that mean?"

"It means you can work with me."

A pleased expression appeared on Ralus' face. "What can I do?"

"You can help me clean and feed the animals. That's enough."

Chapter Six
Bonding

The alarm clock went off the next morning promptly at five-thirty. Karen woke up with a cramp in her leg, and while massaging it, she summoned Guider and asked that the siren be canceled. "I'm already awake."

"Understood," it said and vanished.

Her hamstring still had a number of painful knots in it, so Karen continued her massage then got up to run through her list of mobility exercises once more. Finally limbered up, she nudged Ralus' shoulder. "Hey, let's eat and get to work."

Blinking her eyes owlishly, Ralus wandered over to the bathroom wall and Karen opened it up for her. A yell of, "I'm finished!" prompted her to open it again and she wished that the language-link device would get fixed soon. She didn't feel like opening doors all the time. There were other, more important things to do.

After a simple breakfast of fruit and eggs and after Ralus donned a fresh uniform provided by the ship, Karen reviewed her schedule. Feed the canarians first then the other animals. Scour the enclosures and check on the dragons. She wanted to see how the female was doing.

The tolop showed up as they walked to the lift, and Karen wondered how the little starfish-ray managed to get out of its enclosure so easily. She'd seen the space and it had the same kind of door that all the others had. Since it didn't talk, she labeled its escapes as a mystery to be solved another day. It jumped into her arms, she rubbed its belly, and it mewled. "This is Ralus," she said, and pointed to the younger girl.

With a quick move of its head, the tolop immediately turned to view the new arrival, but gave a sniff and clung to Karen again, making a bleating sound, and its eyes narrowed as if it didn't approve of her.

"It doesn't like me," Ralus said, the corners of her mouth turning downward.

"It likes warm bodies."

A sigh came from the younger girl. "Our people have a very low body temperature. I remember my mother telling me that long ago." At the mention of the word 'mother', her voice caught.

A pang of remorse ran through Karen. Her parents hadn't been gone so long, either. It still hurt to know that they wouldn't be coming back, and for a moment, the memories of the horrific crash passed in front of her eyes. Taking in a deep breath in order to calm down, she nodded in the direction of the lift. "Let's go to work."

The canarians came first, and before entering the enclosure, Karen told Ralus to wait outside. There was only one breather. "Trust me. They're hungry birds."

Sure enough, the birds came swooping down in a quick-rush dive-bomb for food, screaming all the way.

Karen dove for the lever and managed to reach it in time. The seeds poured out, and the birds greedily snapped them up. Once done, they screeched out what seemed to be a thank you and flew off.

"That seemed easy," Ralus commented as Karen exited the enclosure. "Is that all you do here, just feed the animals?"

It seemed to be the only thing. "You can try next time."

While feeding the other animals, something strange occurred. The animals sniffed the air as soon as she entered and seemed warier this time, hanging back and keeping a healthy distance. A few of them snorted and eyed her carefully, but didn't do anything that bordered on aggression.

Yet, when the food came out, they approached it without hesitation. The Malurian dragons seemed especially quiet. The female, now breathing normally, waddled over to Karen after eating and nudged her with its head — gently. That came as surprise.

"They like you," Ralus observed.

This was laughable. "They like food. That's all."

Still, Karen wondered why the dragons had acted that way. Maybe it was because the female was pregnant or something else. In all probability, the study screens had the answer, but she didn't have time to hit the books.

Once the dragons had been fed, cleaning came next, and Ralus took the lead. "Show me how to do this," she said, her eyes shining. "I want to help."

Thinking that things would go faster, Karen decided to give her a simple task. "Okay, here's what you do," she said after tapping the panels and pulling out the buckets, mops and hoses. "You know how to use these, right?"

Ralus grabbed them right away. "I know what to do. We had similar tools like this on my world," she stated with confidence. "Let me try, please?"

"Have fun."

The cycle of feeding and cleaning continued, and once inside the actillion compound, both of the moth-like beings fluttered down to land in front of Karen. They stood there, motionless, and the edges of their wings glittered with lethal metal. It was their eyes, though, that piqued her interest. Black as coal, they were dark and devoid of any emotion save one — curiosity.

Like the dragons, they blinked at her. The smaller of the two flapped its wings, sending a gust of air her way and blowing her hair back. Karen stood stock-still. Was this a greeting or was it an attack? She didn't know, but both of them did the wing-flapping thing and the male, the larger one, nudged her with its leg.

"Uh, hi," Karen said, not knowing what else to do. Part of her felt fear, but the other part — curiosity — won out, and she tentatively put out her hand. They bent down to sniff it, then flew off.

"Weird," she muttered as she left.

Once outside, Ralus observed, "I'm finished. I did a good job of cleaning the cages, didn't I?"

For some reason, the remark irked Karen. "They're not cages," she said. Not that she was into the animals all that much, but she thought it only right to use the proper terminology. "They're enclosures."

Ralus gulped and put her hands to her mouth as if she'd committed a major faux pas. "I'm sorry. I'll remember. What do we do next?"

After consulting her schedule, Karen found nothing more to do, so she looked at the enclosures then at her watch. It was almost one p.m., so she said, "You did a pretty good job with the cleaning. Let's eat. I'll show you what an A-one hamburger is supposed to taste like."

"Is that food?"

"Yes."

Ralus beamed.

* * * *

Dream time, and the hidden memories inside Karen's mind emerged. As a little girl she'd been taught all about somersaults and rolls and flips, courtesy of gymnastics classes that her mother had taken her to.

"Your daughter is a natural," the coach said. "If she keeps progressing, she'll be a winner in any competition she decides to enter."

Karen heard the words of praise, saw her mother's face glow with pride, and dreamed of the day when she'd be the leader at something.

More images, this time of junior high, followed. On the field Karen excelled at gymnastics, running, swimming and anything athletic. A natural, that's what she was, and nothing involving flexibility and strength and speed seemed beyond her. Strong and agile, she had what coaches called innate natural talent and any sport she took up, she owned. There was nothing better, she decided, than being able to run like the wind, throw like a major leaguer and swim like a fish. Glory waited. She just had to reach out and take it, for it had been hers.

In an abrupt shift, her memories skipped forward to the night when everything changed. Freshman year in high school now, it was a time to make new friends and try new things. The cheerleading squad needed some new talent and held a tryout session. Karen passed by the gymnasium while on the way to her locker, saw the other girls do their stuff and knew that she could beat them.

Inside the ladies' room, she primped in front of the mirror and nodded at her image. Only the prettiest and best got to the top and she was ready to do her thing...

"I made the cheerleading team!" she crowed once she got back home.

It had been tough, with ten girls all vying for the final spot, and Karen had nailed it with a triple backflip, a series of somersaults and a jazzy dance routine she'd improvised on the spot. After the two minutes of doing her stuff had been up, all the other girls had crowded around her and given her congratulatory hugs. Talk about a beyond massive ego boost! This was her fifteen minutes of fame, right here and right now.

Her mother, slender and blonde with a quick smile and a cheerful attitude, hugged her in the hallway. "That's great news! I'll tell your father. He'll be home soon."

A few minutes before six, her father walked through the door. On the short side, he also had blond hair and a quiet but fun-loving side. "Well, that is good news," he declared, patting Karen on the shoulder. "Scholar, athlete... I think that deserves sushi."

"Yeah, I'm up for sushi," Karen stated, and ran to the car.

From there, the events unfolded in her mind, the speed of her father's sedan, the turns and smooth movement, the thought that soon she'd be using chopsticks to scarf down salmon and tuna and shrimp-and-avocado rolls and more, then the horror of the approaching car, the screech of the brakes, her father yelling, "Get down," and then...

Darkness fell, but the darkness soon turned to light and she had a pain in her right leg, a monstrous pain, something she'd never experienced before. Once she woke up and found out her parents were dead, once she accepted that she'd never see them again...even now, she still couldn't accept it.

A few days after the operation, a man had come around to see her — she'd put it out of her mind, but it came back now. In his mid-forties, short and slight, he bowed his head as he entered the room. "I'm Jamie Morris' father," *he said.* "William Morris. My son was" — *he paused and wiped a sudden tear from his eye* — "was driving the car that hit you."

Eternity ensued as Karen stared at him, incapable of speech. This man... What did he want, forgiveness? Screw that. "What do you want?" *she finally asked, struggling up to a semi-inclined position.*

Morris had licked dry lips. "I wanted to tell you how sorry I am," *he started off by saying.* "My son...he should have never gotten into his car. He was drunk." *A catch sounded in his voice.* "I didn't know until the police came around to tell me and my wife."

Rage started to build in Karen. This guy has to be kidding. What did he come here for, just to say that he's sorry? *"So what happened to your son?" she asked.* "Does he know he killed my parents? Does he know what happened to me?"

"He died on impact," *Mr. Morris said in a whisper.* "Broken neck...that's what the police told me." *He shook his head as if to rid himself of the sorrow.* "I wasn't sure if I should come here or not."

Karen hadn't thought of herself as a vengeful person, but at that moment a sense of satisfaction swept over her, as the man who'd taken away the only two people who'd ever mattered to her was dead, too. She then looked up to see Mr. Morris weeping.

"I don't know how to ask you to forgive me — or even if you can," *he said between sobs.* "I just came to tell you how sorry I am."

Just as suddenly as she'd been pleased, though, Karen's satisfaction vanished. Hearing the news that Morris had also died, a dull and hollow feeling entered her belly. She hadn't known who this guy was, what he'd liked, where he'd lived or why he'd decided to do what he'd done. She didn't know if he'd been married or if he'd had a girlfriend. And she really didn't feel like asking his father.

In a way, justice had prevailed. The dude had gotten what he deserved, but it didn't change a thing. Her parents were still gone and she was scarred and too damn bad. Life went on.

"If you need money, my insurance company will pay for the hospitalization," Mr. Morris said, interrupting Karen's thoughts. "My wife and I aren't rich, but we'll do what we can to help you start over – "

"No," Karen interrupted. "You don't have to. Nothing's going to bring my parents back. Just…get out and leave me alone."

Morris started to cry once more and slowly shuffled through the doorway. Karen thought about her parents being gone and she too began to sob. They'd always been there for her and now they weren't. She cried until no more tears would come out and then she wondered if she had done the right thing.

It didn't matter. In time, maybe I'll learn to live with how things turned out. "Maybe one day I will," she whispered to no one in particular.

From that point on, all she could do was to get well. "Try and bend your knee," the specialist said. They were in the rehabilitation room, a large, white complex filled with weight machines, large rubber bands used for resistance, massage tables and more. It smelled of sweat and strain, and on the other side of the room, a woman, perhaps in her mid-twenties, sat in a wheelchair, doing pulldowns on a lat machine.

"Try and bend your knee," the specialist repeated. Her therapist, a young man with powerful arms and hands, helped her try to extend and flex her knee then put her *through some weight training drills that hurt more than the flexibility exercises.*

"Push it. Push yourself," he said over and over. "If you want to get back to what you were, you have to work for it."

Karen concentrated, did as he said, and came out of the sessions dripping sweat and sore all over. The only reason she put up with the exercise was that she wanted to walk normally. Also, she had nowhere else to go. Television bored her, and she spent time staring out the window, watching the world pass her by, then she heard the sound of something strange bleating in the night and found the starfish-ray and now she was...

Awake!

Karen sat up and blinked, the sweat pouring off her and her breath coming out in rapid pants. While in the hospital, she'd blamed herself at first. If she hadn't made the cheerleaders' squad they'd never have gone out for dinner. However, she'd come to realize that her parents couldn't have known. They couldn't have foreseen the accident and now they were gone and life went on.

A tear slipped from her eye and she wiped it away along with the sweat. Beside her, Ralus continued to sleep peacefully, a slight smile on her face. At least someone could sleep.

Deciding that a walk might help, Karen went down to the enclosure to check on the animals. They didn't seem perturbed by her presence. The dragons approached the glass, sniffing and snorting away, and she wondered if they were curious or being friendly. Maybe both, so taking a chance, she walked inside. The female watched her, eyes flat and unblinking, while the male ambled over and gave her a gentle nudge with its head.

"So that's your way of saying hello?"

With a slow, careful move, Karen ran her hand over his back. He didn't move a muscle, but she felt his body quivering, as if aching to run or lay a beating on some unfortunate animal. She couldn't tell which.

Out of the corner of her eye, she found the female dragon watching *her*, but the expectant mother made no threatening moves.

"You mind if I borrow the big guy?" Karen asked. In a spur of the moment decision, she hopped on the male's back and grabbed onto the scales as makeshift reins. His body felt like warm iron, and when he moved, his muscles rippled and sent a mini-shockwave up her spine and out the top of her head. "Hey, do you want to walk around?"

The dragon responded by moving along slowly, and she guided him around the enclosure by gently squeezing her knee against his side. "That was pretty cool," she said after hopping off his back onto her good leg. He nudged her with his snout again and turned around to make his way over to his mate, where he settled down beside her.

Outside, Karen breathed a sigh of wonder as well as relief. She'd just made a new friend. "Yeah," she said, and walked over to the actillion moth creatures' enclosure. The moth pair was nowhere to be seen, but then a fluttering sound made her look up. The female flew down to land in front of her, sniffed her and a faint whiff of what seemed to be cedar — or something very close to it — filled the air.

Consulting her pocket guide while never taking her eyes off the massive moth, she heard the computer recite, "The female secretes a glandular substance similar to perfume and pleasant body odors when in the presence of another being it does not fear."

Karen looked up, startled at the information she'd just heard. It sank in and a slow smile spread across her face. "Huh," she said, surprised. "That was pretty cool."

The moth merely regarded her with an air of calm, but the smell seemed to become stronger. With a sudden flapping of her wings, she flew up to join her mate.

A grinding sound, followed by what sounded like an explosion interrupted the feel-good moment. Scant milliseconds later, a shockwave erupted under her feet and threw her to the ground. "What's going on?" she cried.

Guider appeared at her elbow. "We have hit a rock," it said. "We are assessing the damage. Please return to your quarters."

When she got back to her room, she discovered that Ralus was up and awake, her large eyes wide open and her body trembling. She came over and clung to Karen. "I heard a big noise before. Did something blow up?"

Karen didn't know what to do at first. An only child, she had no experience with other kids in this sort of situation, so she clumsily patted Ralus on the shoulder. "Yeah, we did. I mean, we hit a rock. Guider, uh…that metal ball, is going to tell us later, so calm down. Do you want to go to the main bridge?"

"I don't want to be alone."

Quickly, they made their way up top. White filled the entire viewing screen and only that, nothing more. "What happened?" Karen asked. "Guider, are you there?"

"Here." Guider popped in again, juxtaposing its body between her and the screen. "We are trapped."

The news hit Karen like a punch to the gut. "What do you mean *trapped*?"

Guider threw up another projection screen. A picture of the ship caught between three large chunks of ice, each of them easily the size of two square city blocks, sprang into view. "We are here," Guider said, but the picture was self-explanatory. "The rocks have caught us and the impact damaged our main engine."

Sweat began to pour down Karen's face and her heart started to hammer. Ralus began to cry, her chest heaving. "I'm scared," she sobbed out.

"Can you repair it?" Karen asked, as she went over to throw her arm around Ralus' shoulder.

"Yes," it replied, "but preliminary calculations indicate that it will take approximately thirty hours in which to do so. After that, we must cut our way out of here. Our ship's defense mechanisms can be modified to serve as lasers. They may be enough to cut through the ice."

"May...you're talking about you *may* be able to?" Karen asked as she fought to keep from panicking. There was already one person who couldn't take the stress and she didn't want to be number two.

"Correct. We have never encountered this situation before. Therefore, it is unknown whether we will be able to succeed or not."

Wonderful, what else can go wrong?

As if reading her mind, Guider stated, "We have another problem to contend with."

The poachers...it was talking about the poachers. "Are they still out there?"

"This is unknown at the present time. The magnetic interference from the ice rocks makes our sensor readings unreliable at best. We can only hope that they have left to pursue other matters."

"You left out the part of the Malurian dragon being pregnant." Karen fought to keep her voice from becoming frantic, but she couldn't help it. "It's in its second term. You told me that it was supposed to be ready once it got to...to wherever it is we're going," she sputtered.

Guider flew down to go eye to eye with her. "We did not forget. The dragon has *you*."

It vanished, and while it had probably given the remark in order to impart some confidence, she didn't feel very confident at all. Inadequate was a better word. Ralus continued to cry. Right now, Karen wanted to as well, but she kept the stress pent-up, as there was no one else available to act as a guidance counselor. Someone needed to show some courage here.

Privately, she felt terrified at the prospect of being permanently trapped, but all the same, she believed that they'd be able to get out of this prison somehow. If she had to die, preferably it would be in a warm place.

Chapter Seven
Downtime

With the ship still ice-locked, the pattern of cleaning and feeding continued over the next three days. The lights stayed on. There was no disruption of power, but Guider decided to take an extended vacation for the first two days, and no matter how many times Karen asked it to appear, it didn't. She finally figured that it had to be on the job, supervising the self-repair, and maybe all that data inside it kept it too occupied for human contact.

On the third day, Guider popped in while Karen was observing things from the main bridge. Outside, numerous tiny dots of light hit the rocks from all angles. The pictures shifted every so often and showed bits of ice drifting away. "How are you doing that?" she asked Guider.

"We have managed to reconfigure the ship's defense beams into lasers," it answered. "It is slow going at best, but we are making progress."

It then disappeared and Karen continued to stare as the pinpricks of intense light carved out small chunks of ice which then drifted away on the interstellar tides. How long would it all take? Even if they did manage to cut their way out, they still had to travel to Nar, and that meant entering uncharted territory.

Potential for danger or not, she still had a job to do, and for a change, the monkey alarm did not go off. Instead, the alarm clock woke her and starting out of her bed in an instant, wide awake and ready for action, Karen patted Ralus on the shoulder and she woke up. "What is it?" she asked in a drowsy voice.

Karen walked over to the shower room wall and opened it. "Do what you have to do in the shower. Then we eat and go to work."

Down at the enclosures, Ralus tried to feed the canarians, but they pecked at her unmercifully and drove her from the place, screaming their outrage as she dove through the door. "What did I do wrong?" she wailed after tearing off her face mask, tears running down her face.

"I have no idea."

When Karen went inside, right away the birds swooped down, but didn't peck her. Instead, they stood on the floor side by side, like soldiers at attention. "Hey, if you're hungry, then show some manners," she lectured them in a pseudo-schoolmarm's voice.

The canarians flapped their wings and tapped the metal floor with their feet, but made no other threatening moves, and for a change, they didn't scream. After feeding them, Karen came outside and took off her breather.

Ralus' face wore a petulant expression. "They like you better," she accused, kicking the side of the enclosure and stomping off in a rage.

"Yeah, they do," Karen said, wondering why. With the exception of the tolop that accompanied them almost everywhere, the records said nothing about friendliness or approachability of the other animals. They just gave the facts and nothing more.

She met Ralus at the ovidian enclosure. The younger girl was sitting on the ground, head down. Karen didn't have to look to know that she was pouting. "Hey," she said, putting on a friendly air, "if you have a problem, you can talk to me."

"You're the problem," Ralus answered in a shaky voice. "The animals, they hate me."

A wave of sympathy flowed through Karen. Her first couple of days here hadn't been much different. "No, they just don't know you. I don't know why they're into me. I guess they're just used to me is all. You, uh... I guess you have to gain their confidence. Talk to them. Pet them if they'll let you."

Viewing the situation, things had changed completely. If they were going to make it out of here, then they all had to get along. "Look...uh...didn't you have any animals you kept on your home planet, like pets or something?"

It was risky to bring the topic up so soon, but Karen felt that she had to try something. Ralus wasn't a bad kid. She'd lost everything, and when a person lost everything, sometimes they lost the will to go on.

Ralus shook her head. "My parents were farmers, and they were always busy. On my planet, we stayed at home and studied about farming and other boring stuff. We lived in the countryside, and the nearest farm was a long way away. Only the scientists lived in the cities. They built our machines and interstellar radios. That's what my parents told me."

Curious, Karen asked her how old she was. "I've seen almost thirteen seasons," Ralus replied. "My little sister saw only six of them. I sometimes played games with her, but she couldn't play them well. She liked to play in the garden and I liked to stay inside, so that's what I did most of the time."

In a sudden shift, her face twisted with grief and her lower lip began to tremble. "You...asked me about a pet. We had something called a varaan," she said. "It was soft and cuddly, but"—her voice shook even more—"but it's gone now. Everything is gone."

With that, she broke down entirely, and Karen did the only thing she could do. She put her arms around the younger girl and held her until the shaking stopped. "Hey, I've been there," she said. "I never had a pet, but I lost my parents, too."

Ralus looked up at her with a tear-stained face. "You...did?"

"Yeah, I did. And I didn't lose them so long ago, either."

Haltingly, Karen recounted the whole story, as much as she could remember. As she spoke, she tried not to get angry at the unfairness of it all then realized—just as she'd realized in the hospital—that you had to be fair in life. What had happened wasn't Ralus' fault any more than it was hers.

After finishing off her story of how her injuries came to be, Karen pointed at her leg and then at her face. "This is what happened, why I walk sort of funny and I look sort of funny."

Ralus put up her hand to gently run her fingers around the edges of the scar. "I didn't know," she said after a time. "I thought, maybe, that your people used that as a mark, or you were born with it. It's pretty deep, though."

The remark stung and Karen's temper flashed.

"Yeah, it's deep and it's ugly." She would have to be reminded of her injury. Why not hold up a mirror and let her see the damage?

"I'm sorry..." Ralus started to say.

Words, born of frustration, tumbled from Karen's lips and she chopped the air.

"Hey, I didn't ask for this. I didn't ask to have my leg shattered. I didn't ask to be marked for life. I wanted to do just what everyone else did, go bike riding and run and maybe meet a nice guy and go on dates. I wanted to be normal!"

Abruptly she exploded with, "I didn't ask to be kidnapped, either. And no, I *don't* like the way I look, so if you're going to give me the I-don't-think-you're-ugly routine, then don't. I know what I look like."

Totally deflated, she dropped her arms at her sides, chest still heaving with muted rage. The urge to cry came over her and she turned her head away and fought it off. Crying was for babies.

She then felt a hand tap her arm and swiveled her gaze back to find Ralus staring at her, her eyes wet.

"I'm sorry if I hurt you," said Ralus in a soft voice. "I didn't think I was saying anything wrong. I've never seen a human before."

Let it go. Ralus hadn't meant anything cutting or bad, not like the others. Not like the head of the cheerleading squad, Susan Meacham, who'd come in her three days after the accident. She'd taken one look and said, "Like, that's the biggest scar around. Guess you're not coming back in the fall, are you?"

The other girls on the team had hastily pulled her out of the room. Karen had curbed her desire to say something mean, split her in two with a vicious comeback, but the mirror had showed that Susan, bitchy attitude or not, happened to be right. There had been external scars and internal ones. Which had hurt more was debatable.

Switching back to the here and now, Karen blew out a deep breath. *Let it go.* It wasn't worth getting angry over, not anymore. "Forget it. You didn't mean anything by it at all. C'mon. Let's get something to eat."

* * * *

Day three brought a little relief. Inside the actillions' enclosure, the giant moths flitted down to look at both of them, their beady eyes dancing back and forth. Finally, the female leaned down to smell Ralus and the girl exclaimed, "They smell sweet!"

A distinct wave of pleasure hit Karen and she grinned. "That means they like you."

It seemed to be a bit more than like, for Ralus ran around to the female's side and the moth used the flat part of her wing to lift the girl up onto her back.

"Oh wow," Karen breathed. "Uh, hang on!" The information screens hadn't said anything about this.

The moth flapped its wings and slowly rose into the air. An apprehensive expression crossed Ralus' face, but it then changed to one of joy as the moth flew around the wide airspace and she shouted out, "This is great!"

"Yeah," Karen murmured, transfixed by the scene. "It is."

After landing, the giant moth waved its wing in Karen's direction. She got on, hung on to the fur of its back — it was surprisingly soft — and they soared aloft. The moth let out a pleasant chirping sound as it banked left and right. A rush of wind blew her hair back, and Karen got a moth's eye view of the zoo park as she flew by the window. "Keep flying!" she yelled. The feeling was indescribably fantastic, as if she could reach out and touch the sky.

Unfortunately, the ride ended all too soon. The moth circled slowly toward the ground and landed lightly on its feet, Karen slid off its back and fell as she landed on her bad leg. She looked up just in time to see the actillion fly away. As she got to her feet, Ralus skipped over and they gave each other a brief hug. "I want to see more of the animals!" Ralus cried.

"We can do that."

And so it went. Karen had the ship fashion a pair of sunglasses and she placed them on the Malurian dragon so that he wouldn't freak out in the bright sunlight. His skin turned yellow, but he allowed both of them to get onto his back without incident.

"Let's get ready to rumble," Karen said with a smirk.

"What does that mean?"

Simplify, simplify... "Uh, it means, let's ride."

"Oh."

It didn't take more than a few minutes to teach her how to ride the animals, and while Ralus went off on her own adventure, Karen checked on the female. Her information screen didn't tell her much about how to treat the pregnancy, but apparently, the dragons were used to giving birth on their own—had done so for millennia—so she decided to let nature take its course.

As for the other animals, she made the decision to open up the enclosures. "Is this a smart thing to do?" Ralus asked her, as the animals ambled out into the open air.

"No, probably not," Karen answered. She didn't like the idea of the animals being caged up. If this was a zoo—alien or not—she thought it better that the animals roam free. They were drugged up, anyway, and seemed calm enough.

After letting them out, those that liked sunshine sniffed the air and began to move around. They also sniffed each other, but outside of a few snorts and grunts, none of them seemed in a combative mood. The actillion moths flew down and Ralus immediately ran over to the female, taking off and yelling with joy, while Karen rode on the back of the dragon. He galloped around this time and at a high speed, too, and she thought it like a wild buggy ride.

Once done, she slid off and walked in front to give him a gentle rub on its head. In the back of her mind, Karen remembered Guider's caution about the animals' instincts taking over, but oddly enough, she felt no fear. A second after the rubbing stopped, he shot out a nose rocket and part of it splashed her on her forearm. By now she was used to the odor.

"That smells!" Ralus cried.

The dragon obliged Karen by dousing Ralus in nose spray. "Now so do you," Karen grinned. "You'll live."

Time passed with the animals doing the search-and-sniff routine, and Karen suddenly got tired and wondered how the repairs were progressing. "Okay, guys," she called out. "You have to go home."

At first, the creatures didn't move, so Karen took them back to their cages, approaching them carefully and leading them back with a gentle, but firm, hand. They obeyed, which mystified yet gratified her no end.

Once they were safely inside, she and Ralus made their way to the bridge. The viewing screen showed a clear path out of the ice field. Guider decided to pop in then and announced, "Karen, we are ready to leave."

Good news seemed to be on the forecast today, she thought. "Are we going to Nar?"

The ball bobbed up and down. "We cannot, not yet. We must make a brief stop at Delberon. We were only recently contacted. The people there have been under attack and wish to give us one of their animals."

She breathed out a sigh. "I don't suppose you have the data on them?"

"We do not. We should be arriving at Delberon in roughly two hours."

Guider then vanished. The question of whether she should tell the Keepmasters about letting the animals out rang in her mind, but she figured that they probably wouldn't appreciate her actions. *Better to keep silent.*

Ralus pulled on her arm. "Can we get something to eat?"

"Good idea," Karen responded, and they went off to the commissary to eat. As they munched on egg sandwiches, she realized that interstellar travel between worlds consisted of boredom. Staring out at the stars wasn't her thing. Since the ship had the ability to manufacture playing cards, she'd teach Ralus. It would help to pass the time.

* * * *

When they landed on Delberon, Guider appeared at the exit and said that the planet's atmosphere was thin, but breathable. "From the preliminary scans we have done, it appears that the people here are similar to reptiles. The air will be like that of a mountaintop. Please be careful."

Guider's tone sounded worried, and Karen felt no less worried. "Ralus, you stay here."

"I want to help," Ralus begged. "This animal may be heavy and I can help you lift it. Please?"

This whole take-me-along bit was asking for trouble, Karen believed, but figured that they were probably going to have to take back at least two animals, so she relented. "Okay, you can come, but stay close to me. Don't get into trouble."

"I won't."

Ralus actually grinned as if she'd been told they were going to have a picnic. The door opened, and the gangplank went down into a puddle of mud. It splashed on her, and appeared slimy and thick. "Gross," she muttered.

The gangplank led directly into a swamp. Stagnant water was everywhere with a thick coating of greenish mold on top. In the few places where land sprouted, it was covered in the mud. Karen walked carefully and still managed to slip a few times. Good thing that Ralus stuck by her side and helped steady her as they walked down a narrow spit of land.

Along the way, Karen felt her lungs beg for air. It took a couple of minutes to make the initial adjustment, and her heart sped up to keep pace with the more difficult aspects of breathing. The sky above was a dismal grayish-black, and heavy, fat raindrops spattered them. The rain smelled as bad as the mud did.

As they trod along, the sky grew darker, and here and there some trees made an appearance, most of them over twenty feet high, but also horribly stunted and blackened. A fine black mist hung in the air, making it hard to see. "So where are the people?" Ralus asked. She didn't seem to have any problems with her breathing.

"Hello there," a voice said, and off to the left, two men stood, each of them carrying a small cage.

Guider happened to be right, Karen thought. At roughly seven feet in height and strongly built, they resembled crocodiles more than anything else. With long snouts and blood-red eyes, they were green all over and wore what looked to be metal armor. In addition to carrying the cages, they also had guns hanging from their belts.

Ralus shied back, but Karen grabbed her and told her to stay where she was. "Don't be rude. They're our hosts, and we have to make a good impression," she hissed.

"They are scary to look at."

If ever someone needed an attitude adjustment, Karen thought, now was the time. "What...? I'm a cover model, is that right?"

"What's a cover model?"

Patience, Karen remembered. She had to have patience. "It's a very pretty woman. I'm not pretty." She pointed at her scar. "Remember?"

"Yes, but you don't look like them."

Rubbing her mark, Karen attempted to keep her temper down. "We're not here to date them," she said in a sharp voice. "We're just here to take the animals they have and that's all, so be quiet, okay?"

Ralus nodded, and her face wore a chastened expression. "I'm sorry. I'll be quiet."

"Good."

As the men approached, she looked around them warily. One of them spoke to her in a high, reedy voice. "We contacted your people. We are sorry to ask on such short notice, but our planet has been under attack by some pirates, and we need to protect these animals."

"What are they called?" Ralus asked.

Karen stifled the urge to say "Oh will you learn to shut it?" Instead, she pulled back and asked sharply, "Who's in charge here?"

Ralus clamped her lips shut, but before doing so, whispered, "You are."

Darn right I am. She turned to the crocodile men. "I'm sorry," she said, offering a smile. "She's new here. What are they called?" she added, pointing at the cages.

"They are called sarkus," the first man said. "They are the rarest of our animals and there are very few of them left. We have been recently invaded, and the pillagers are here now. We must be on the alert."

He handed her his cage and she peered at the occupant inside. With long, blond hair, the animal resembled a Peruvian guinea pig, as it had the same size and shape, but it had long legs instead of stubby ones, and it stood a good seven inches above the cage's bottom. It also had enormous ears which were twice the size of its body.

Topping the different looks department off, it also had abnormally long and curved fangs, very lethal looking ones. It looked like a mix of a mini-elephant, a rodent and a vampire, and Karen fought down a sudden urge to giggle. "It's sort of cute," she said.

"Hurry, please," the second man said, handing his cage over to Ralus. "The enemy is almost upon us, and—"

He never got to finish his sentence as a bolt of blue lightning came out of nowhere and vaporized him. A second shot destroyed the other man, and Ralus yelped in fear.

"Don't move," a voice said. The figure stepped out from behind one of the trees, a gun in his hand. The voice sounded familiar and Karen cursed herself for being caught out in the open. Still, it hadn't been anyone's fault. Guider couldn't have known, as the poachers had probably cloaked their ship. "Move and you die."

The figure approached them, and from the way it was built—immensely fat as well as heavily muscled in its legs—she knew it was Blaron. He approached cautiously, looking off to his left then to his right, and satisfied that no one else was around, he tucked the gun into his waist belt. "What is your name, girl?"

Karen fought down her fear and replied, "Karen, Karen Fox."

The poacher smiled at her, revealing black and rotting teeth. Why all the bad guys had to have bad teeth, she wondered, was beyond her. And he also suffered from a severe case of body odor. He smelled worse than the snot from the Malurian dragons. Or maybe that was how all his people smelled. If so, she pitied them. "I see you have a friend with you, carrying what belongs to me."

"Her name is Ralus," Karen answered, wondering if she was fast enough to grab the gun on his belt. And if she did, what would she do with it? Simply hold him hostage? "And these animals don't belong to you."

A hoarse laugh came from him and made his belly shake. "Girl, I recognize the child standing beside you. I must admit, it gave me tremendous pleasure to destroy her world."

Karen stole a look at Ralus, who was trembling with fear as well as having a look of supreme hatred in her eyes. "Hang tough," she whispered, then realizing that slang wasn't appropriate in this situation, added, "Be brave."

Blaron didn't blink at all and she felt the power of his gaze. "You may counsel her all you wish," he said, "but the reality is that I have ten men standing behind me and we all possess weapons. Moreover, I have the ability to kill anyone I choose, that and the will to do so. You, on the other hand, look to be a mere girl. You are pretty enough, though, facial scar and physical infirmity notwithstanding."

"How did you…?" she began.

A thin slit of a smile formed on his mouth. "We have had you under surveillance from the moment you touched down in that most impressive ship of yours. We know how you walk, how you talk and what you are here for."

With a massive paw, he reached up to leisurely scratch his unshaven face. His fingers were thick, stained black and cracked and lined, but they looked powerful enough to tear someone's head off. "You might do well to stay with me, marked though you are. You are of age, are you not?"

He would have to mention me being scarred up. Karen reacted angrily, but revulsion soon replaced the anger. *He wants me as his girlfriend? Oh, no way to that!*

The notion sent a shudder of distaste through her. This man was slime personified. "First off, I'm sixteen. That's a little young for you. Second, I'm not interested. Third, you aren't getting these animals. If you try anything, I'll let them go. Try catching them."

This time Blaron did blink and a flicker of fear showed in his eyes. "You...you would not let them go here, would you?"

Why was he so afraid, Karen wondered, unless...unless these little critters were dangerous? Well, they *did* have fangs. It was time to find out. "Ralus," she said while still looking at the pig-man, "when I give the order, open the cage."

By this time, the remainder of Blaron's men, all of them fat and porcine looking like their leader, had come out of their hiding places to stand behind him, but at Karen's command, they started to back up. Blaron held up his fist and they halted. "Girl, if you value your life and that of the child who stands beside you, then you will not do this. These are valuable animals and will fetch a high price. I do not wish to chase after them. You had better not open those cages."

Karen grinned. "How much do you want to bet?"

Blaron snapped his fingers. One of the other pig-men stepped forward. "Bring out the specimen." He pointed to the cage Karen was holding.

That proved to be a mistake. Once the poacher opened the door, the sarkus moved in a surprising burst of speed as it reached out its long claws, clamped them on either side of the man's head, and proceeded to bite it off.

"Holy crap, that's...!" Karen exclaimed, and stopped right there. It seemed no other words would do.

Ralus gasped and Karen stared as blood fountained out of the stump and the beheaded poacher's body quivered like a headless chicken's. It did a brief crazy dance of death and then the corpse fell into the nearest swamp where it sank from view.

"You little witch!" Blaron cried. "Do you know what you've done?"

"I let the dogs out," Karen replied, as she fought down the urge to hurl. Quickly, she shut the cage's door. "You want some more?" She forced a smile, but the poachers obviously didn't possess a sense of humor. "I'm guessing that the sarkus can fly and they're probably hungry. So who's next?"

The rest of the lackeys got the idea and hauled their butts out of the combat zone. Mission accomplished, Karen stood tall and held the cage in front of her, her hand on the latch.

Only Blaron remained behind, and he was beside himself with rage, stomping and swearing loud enough for the entire quadrant to hear. "That man," he snarled. "He was my brother!"

Instead of feeling sorry about it, Karen brandished her cage and kept her hand on the lock. Anger flowed through her unchecked. "Yeah, accent the past tense," she said. "He *was* your brother. You murdered a world and it looks like you want to kill this one, too. But here" — she gently shook the cage — "I've got the game changer, and last I looked, there was just one of you and two of them. How fast can you draw?"

Blaron's fury caused his eyes to turn blood red and he made a quick move in her direction, his hand going for his gun. With a roundhouse swing, she smacked him in the face with the cage and he lost his balance, falling clumsily to the ground. The gun clattered off into the nearby swamp and immediately disappeared from view. "Guess you can't draw very fast, can you?" she taunted. "Now get out."

Slowly, he got to his feet, cursing her name, her family's name, the ship she was on, and more. Nonstop obscenities poured from his mouth and he moved to the tree line in order to deliver a parting shot. "Karen Fox, fortune smiles upon you this time. We shall meet again. I will remember your face, the face of your Platusian friend and the humiliation of today."

"I'll try to forget you," she answered as nonchalantly as possible. "It won't be easy, but I'll give it my best shot." She motioned for Ralus to get going. The younger girl wheeled around and sprinted toward the ship.

Spinning around on her heel, Karen limped as fast as she could and soon got to the ship. Guider met them at the entrance.

"Hurry up and take off," she said, heading for the enclosure. "Those poachers are very, very angry."

"As you wish," it said.

Karen motioned for Ralus to follow her to the elevator. She heard the comforting thrumming sound of the engines and felt the ship shift. It was a smooth, unlabored kind of movement, and the farther away from this place, the better.

It took only a few seconds to get to the animal park. Once there, Karen found the enclosures for their cargo and opened the cage doors. Immediately, the little vampire creatures flew inside and settled down. She heaved a sigh of relief after shutting the doors, but as she did so, a sudden chill ran through her. Blaron's brother was dead. He most definitely would *not* forget this overnight.

"What shall we do now?" Ralus asked. She was still upset, and her lower lip trembled.

It wouldn't do to show any fear in front of the girl, Karen decided, and gave her a thumbs up. "We relax. Let's go back to my room."

Once inside, she plopped down and put her bad leg over a cushion, letting out a satisfied grunt. Ralus sat beside her. "What does that mean?" she wanted to know. She imitated the thumbs-up gesture.

"What, the sign?" Karen asked. "It means you did a good job and you handled yourself well."

Ralus gave her a smile. It seemed that she was pleased at getting complimented for doing something adult in nature. She said, "I think I'll take a short rest," and promptly fell asleep.

Karen drew the blanket over her, but there was no way that she could sleep, though—not now. She was too troubled by the appearance of the poachers. They'd been on Delberon, had a faster ship, and didn't care about other forms of life at all. They wouldn't give up so easily now.

Guider popped in again. "Haven't seen you around too much," Karen remarked. "What happened?"

The little ball bobbed up and down as if acknowledging her point. "We must apologize, Karen, but the repairs to the ship's structure and engines as well as the medicinal dispensary systems took priority. We trust that there were no problems in our absence?"

"You mean you didn't know about the poachers?"

"We did not. Their cloaking device works better than ours does. It was impossible to find them. We are sorry, but we are also most gratified that you and Ralus are well."

If ever there was a time to get angry, it was now, but she figured that it wasn't worth it. She also wondered if they'd been monitoring her bonding with the animals. "Uh, were you following me around when I was on duty?"

"No, we were otherwise occupied."

Bonus time, she thought. Part of her wanted to do her happy dance, but the other part of her told her to cool it for now. Guider hadn't seen her and Ralus playing with the animals. This *was* some pretty hot news.

"Oh, okay," she said, attempting to sound nonchalant. "Uh, well, I showed Ralus what to do and we just fed the animals, cleaned up...the usual stuff..."

Abruptly she stopped talking as something that Guider had said came back to her. "What's this about the dispensary systems?"

The reply came immediately. "When the ship was damaged, the system that administers the drug to the animals' food was also disrupted."

"What drug are you talking about?"

"The drug that dulls the more violent animals," Guider replied. "The drugs have not been administered, and in any case, their effects wear off after only a few hours. Such is the nature of the species we carry. Please be careful when feeding them. Excuse us, please. We are on course for Nar and will be there in roughly four hours."

Guider disappeared and Karen went back to her room, her mind whirling with the possibilities. The animals hadn't been drugged. They should have acted like they did on their home worlds...but didn't. "Karen, what's wrong?" Ralus asked her when she entered. "You look worried."

"I do?"

Ralus' eyes grew round. "Yes, you do. Did something happen?"

"No…just that we're going to Nar," Karen replied.

As she sat down and tried to relax, Karen thought about what Guider had told her. Trust was a two-way street and had to be earned. Right now, it seemed as though she'd earned the right to call the animals her friends, and that notion, abstract as it was, made her feel very positive.

Chapter Eight
Nar

"I have gin rummy!" Ralus cried and smacked her cards down on the floor.

Karen sighed and mentally chalked up another win for her opponent, figuring that she'd already lost around two million dollars by now. When would they land?

Guider had been right. The universe was infinitely huge, something that boggled the imagination. Since neither of them had had anything better to do after finishing their chores, Karen had decided to teach Ralus about card games, Earth's monetary system and other basic facts. The younger girl showed an astonishing ability to not only learn extremely fast but also to consistently win at gin rummy.

Who was the card-master here, anyway? Karen had never been defeated by anyone and now that she was on the losing end, she didn't like it one bit. To mask her disappointment, she turned to showing off some magic and Ralus was astonished.

"We don't have that kind of game on my world," she said. "Is it popular back on your planet?"

"With some people it is. I do it to pass the time."

Ralus still couldn't get the sleight of hand movements, no matter how slowly they were done. "How can you do that?" she asked.

"Practice," Karen shrugged.

They went back to playing gin rummy, and while taking a card from the deck, Ralus asked, "Do you have a life-friend?"

Karen was rearranging her cards and looked up. "What?"

"A life-friend," Ralus repeated. "It means a person who is important to you."

While thinking about how to answer, Karen continued to arrange her cards. After the accident, no one, save Ron, had ever bothered really visiting or stuck around. She'd never had a whole lot of friends when younger, either, but she'd had her parents, and now…now what did she have? She had a starfish-ray that liked to sleep with her, a dragon that shot nose rockets at her on a daily basis, a pseudo little sister who was a good gin rummy player and not a whole lot else. A memory of the one possible boyfriend swam up in her mind.

Jim Caldwell, big, built and good-looking, stopped in at the hospital. Karen had gone out with him to the movies a few times, liked him, thought him a possible boyfriend – she'd never had one before – and was glad he turned up. "Hey, how's it going?" he asked, the corners of his mouth shifting up and down in an uncertain smile.

"I've been better."

"Yeah, well, I thought I should come by," he stammered out. "I mean, everyone said you got racked up bad and…"

He didn't say much else, but his eyes lingered on the large bandage covering the right side of her face. Karen caught the stare. "This is what I look like," she said with sudden anger and ripped off the bandage.

Jim's face turned white and when she looked in his eyes, she saw disgust. "Hey, well, it's not so bad," he stammered out in a pseudo-friendly way. "Um, listen, I've got football practice. See you later."

BS excuse given, he practically ran through the door and Karen tossed the bandage at him. "Hope you run into the goalposts!" she yelled, angry tears coursing down her face and stinging her eyes…

"No, there's no one," Karen finally said, her mind coming back to the present. "But you're pretty cool."

Ralus smiled shyly and they continued to play until a gentle bump and all stoppage of movement indicated that the ship had landed. Karen gathered up the cards and shoved them into her uniform. "Let's go."

Guider met them at the exit. "Here you will need a breather, Karen. The atmosphere of this planet is similar to what would be pure ammonia in your world. It will not harm your skin, as you are protected by your uniform, but breathing in this atmosphere will kill you within a few minutes."

A breather sat on the wall, so Karen donned it and waited for the door to open. "I want to go with you," Ralus begged.

"Not this time," Karen answered. "I'm better off alone. Wait here, okay?"

Ralus pouted. "I'll wait."

Guider flew down to hover near the door. "This time the negotiations will be somewhat different than usual. You must go to their village. The Narrians are warlike people and they have only recently accepted our peace plan, but you must show them that you are not only capable, but also gifted."

What was going on here? *Right, I get to deal with more lunacy.* "And just how am I supposed to show them I'm talented?" she asked. "I can't sing. I can't run fast, and I'm not in the mood to show them my cheerleading moves." As if to underscore her words, she rubbed her bad leg. Doubtful she'd be able to cheer and dance, anyway. "So what do these people look like?"

In answer, Guider emitted a hologram and the sight of what appeared to be a Neanderthal, except much larger, appeared in front of her. Perhaps eight feet tall, the picture showed someone with furry skin, vaguely apelike features and a prognathous brow and chin. "Do not let their appearance fool you, Karen," Guider said. "They are highly intelligent, but also extremely suspicious of outsiders. As I said, you must prove your worth."

Fine, Karen thought sourly. She'd figure out something.

After donning the breather, Karen opened the door to a world of twilight. She pulled on a pair of gloves to protect her hands just in case and stepped out onto dry, hard land, somewhat like a desert. This desert also had a number of large rock formations dotting the landscape. She squinted, but couldn't make out much in the dim light.

"Is this world always dark?" she asked Guider.

"Apparently it is. Perhaps one of the inhabitants will have a light source."

Karen scuffed the ground with the toe of her shoe. Her feet threw up small puffs of dust. "Uh, how long will the oxygen last in this breather?" she asked.

"You have approximately three hours," Guider said as the door closed. "It will beep when the supply begins to run out."

"Wonderful," she muttered.

Two figures approached her in the distance, carrying three-foot-long metal poles that emitted halos of light. Like the picture Guider had provided, they were tall, impressively muscled and very hairy, their bodies covered by rough-looking smocks. "You are from the rescuer's party?" one of them asked once they came within range.

"Uh, yeah, that's right," Karen answered. "I'm supposed to pick up two snakes?"

"Come with us."

Just like that—no friendly greeting—so shrugging, Karen followed them down a path, and after a twenty-minute hike, they came upon a small collection of buildings that looked like they'd been quickly patched together from rock, concrete, steel and whatever other materials were on hand. Debris littered the area and there were a number of holes in the uneven terrain. Everything looked very primitive, but after going inside the first building with her hosts, she saw a number of machines and realized that looks were indeed deceptive.

Lights, similar to the ones they carried, lit the room, throwing off a friendly yellow glow. The lead Neanderthal pointed out the interstellar radio, some chemicals they used for medicine and a number of other machines. A large, battered table sat in the center of the room with some crudely constructed wooden chairs around it.

"We apologize for the appearance of our world," he said. "We have recently had a number of battles here, as well as a number of incursions from outsiders, so we are still in the process of rebuilding. It must be strange for you, but this is our way. Please sit and we will talk."

Karen took a seat and tried to figure out how much air she had left. By her calculations, she had roughly two and a half hours. She just hoped that a deal could be made within that time frame. The man who'd guided her in introduced himself as Clodda. "I am the leader of my people. We understand that you will take care of our hebiran for us."

"Uh, yes, that's the deal. The Keepmasters are a good bunch and, uh, we have the enclosures ready. At least, that's how my boss explained it."

He nodded. "We are prepared to trust them, even though we do not trust so easily. However, before we hand over our treasure, we would like a demonstration of your gifts."

What did showing off talent—any kind of talent— have to do with taking care of animals, she wondered. Yet, she didn't say a word. This was how things worked around here, wonky as it sounded.

"What did you have in mind?" she asked.

Clodda rubbed his oversized chin. "We prize talent above all. That is a big part of our culture. Some of our people are skilled in combat while others are talented at crafts or hunting. Have you any ability in any field?"

At a loss, Karen started to say that she didn't, but her hand brushed against her pocket and she remembered the cards that she'd stuffed there. "Would you like to see a trick?"

Clodda blinked and a look of curiosity settled over his face. "Show us."

Taking out the pack, Karen briefly explained the purpose of card games then began to slowly shuffle the deck. She used both hands at first then cut the deck with one hand like a Vegas blackjack dealer would. That task done, she told them that she'd prove herself in terms of magic. "Pick a card," she said.

A few other men wandered in and they watched as she fooled the participants time and again. Smiles from the group broke out. They seemed truly amazed and clapped their hands in appreciation. Karen accepted the compliments with a tiny grin, and when they asked her about how she did it, she replied, "A good magician never reveals her tricks."

It also helped that she'd marked the deck...but they didn't have to know.

Clodda smiled his admiration. "You are indeed gifted."

Karen was pleased, but also had been counting the minutes since she'd arrived. By her estimation, she had around two hours of air left and didn't want to overdo the hospitality thing. "So...have I proved myself to you?"

In answer, he snapped his fingers and one of his men ran off, returning a few moments later with two small cages. "Here. These are our prizes."

Peering inside one of the cages, she saw a small snake barely six inches in length, black all over with a golden dot on the crown of its head, and tiny fangs. It didn't look any different from a snake on Earth. "Uh, not to be rude, but we have snakes like this where I come from. Why is this so special?"

Clodda smiled. "It is not the snake, but its skin. It sheds its skin three times yearly and it can be used to make a medicine that cures certain diseases among not only our people, but among the people of other worlds as well. The snakes are very rare, so rare that it is said that only the fortune of an entire world would be worth buying one. We think of them as a planetary treasure..."

A whistle overhead caused him to stop speaking, and the whistle transitioned into the sound of an explosion nearby. Scant seconds later, the sound of shouting galvanized everyone into action. Clodda arose and ran out the door, returned a moment later and urged Karen to get off her chair.

"We must leave here now!" He went to a corner in the room and grabbed a long, hollow tube. "This will protect us." He shouldered the weapon. "We must go."

Alarmed, Karen rose from her seat. "What's going on?"

"The raiders have come!"

Clodda grabbed her arm and pulled her out the door. "I've got to get back to my ship," she said as they ran along. His soldiers stayed in front of him and they all carried the same tubes. For big men, they moved fast. Her bad leg, though, didn't want to cooperate. In fact, it complained every step of the way, but she was in no position to say anything.

"Our people have told us that the path back to your vessel has been blocked off," he said, puffing. "We shall have to go another route."

The question was where. Clodda stayed out in front then knelt on the ground. He pulled his weapon up, sighted it and let loose a shot in the darkness. A second later, she saw a bright light flare and the sound of an explosion, but heard no other sounds. There was nothing but rocks and dust here, and if the enemy was close...

A shot kicked up the dust in front of her feet. She stopped, and another blast of something yellow came from nowhere and hit Clodda square in his chest. He fell to the ground, and more shots came from out of the darkness to nail the other men.

"Stop right there!" a voice rang out.

She knew that voice. It was Blaron.

"What do you want?" she yelled back.

He stepped out from behind a formation of rocks holding a light-rod in one hand. In the other, he held a very large gun. "I want the snakes and your death," he said. "Let us see which will give me more pleasure."

Blaron's men grabbed her roughly by the arms and shoved her inside one of the buildings and into a chair. "The Narrians are wily and fierce fighters," he said, as he took his place on another chair next to her and turned to his men. "Guard this place well while I entertain my...guest." After they left, he swiveled around to face her. A sudden smile which showed his rotting teeth sent a shudder down her spine.

"You could take the snakes and just leave," Karen suggested in a hopeful voice. They hadn't been here very long—maybe ten minutes—but to her, every breath was precious and she tried very hard not to hyperventilate.

"I could, but I will not. Not yet, at any rate." He shrugged as he tapped his massive fingers on the table, sending up a rattling sound. "I notice that you are wearing a breathing device. You will note that I am not. My people have no need of them. We are very adaptable. This air is pure sweetness to me."

He reached over suddenly and pulled on her breather. Her hands came up instinctively to slap his away. "Don't touch me," she spat.

Blaron chuckled. Coming from him, it sounded like a rusty saw mating with an equally rusty can. "I could take you right now if I wished," he said. "But I will not. I could rip off that breather you wear, but I will not. And do you know why?"

She knew, but decided to ask him anyway. "Okay, tell me why."

"I want to see you suffer."

"What do you know about it?"

He fell silent, drumming his meaty fingers on the table. At length, he spoke again, his voice quiet. "My world is very far from here, located in the farthest quadrant of this galaxy. We are a poor people, one neglected by nature and by that which created us. Our resources are few, our population hungry, and our lives nasty, brutal and short."

Where was all this leading? "So you go out and steal? You kill for the money. Is that it?" Karen asked, trying to buy time, but knowing that time for her was in very short supply. "Why don't you make a deal with the Keepmasters or the other worlds?"

"We have made deals with others over the years," he replied in a nonchalant manner, his fingers still tapping the table rhythmically. "We supply those who will pay for what we take. It is a business and nothing more. We take what we need, receive our share of the wealth from the sales of various creatures then continue. That is our life. Because you are so young, you do not know what it is to suffer."

Karen kept silent. She'd suffered enough, she thought—suffered losing her parents to a drunk who'd made a bad decision, suffered the loss of friends and her life back on Earth, but she doubted that he'd be interested in hearing her tale of woe.

"My life hasn't been all that wonderful," she decided to say.

Blaron stopped his drumming and picked at his teeth. One of them was loose and he pulled it out without a second's hesitation, stared at it then tossed it away. The sight of him doing that made Karen want to gag. No, check that, she thought. Merely *looking* at him made her want to gag. "That was incredibly gross."

"This is not a mission to teach good manners, child," he said in a calm manner. "As for your life not being perfect, I am well aware that you are lame and scarred. It was due to an accident, yes?"

Being reminded of the truth hit her hard, but Karen forced herself to keep calm and focused on his ugly face. "Yes."

He nodded. "Then it is possible that you know something of loss. When I was a boy, I was told by my father that our world was once part of a collective. Whether that is true or not, I do not know, but if so, for one reason or another, we were not allowed the riches enjoyed by other planets in our star system. My father was a craftsman. My mother…I did not know her. She died soon after my brother was born. We grew up in squalor, beaten by other children, but though we suffered, we had each other."

His eyes turned dark. Something lurked there, she saw — something evil. "My brother was all I had. We had a father, but that was in name only as he was nothing but a wastrel. He neglected us, but my brother and I freely shared what we owned and that was precious little. We played together, grew up together, fought together and started our empire together."

He leaned forward and his voice matched his eyes in darkness and intensity. "You say that you know of loss. Due to you, I have no brother. Your life means nothing to me!"

With a swift movement he seized her by the throat. Karen choked under his grip and thrashed around, beating at his hands, but he was far too strong. "I could slay you in the blink of an eye, but that would be too quick and all too easy. It would also give me little satisfaction."

Shoving her away, Karen fell back in her chair, gasping for what little air remained. "Rest assured, I will not kill you now," he said, his voice back to its former quiet level. "I will wait until your supply of oxygen runs out. Then I will watch you as you fight for breath, writhe in exquisite pain, and finally expire."

He got up and shoved his chair back. Going to the door, he opened it and said, "Enjoy what breaths you can take. Very soon you will have none left."

He left, slamming the door shut behind him and Karen started to sob. The thought of the ship so close and yet so far made her weep harder. Conserve air, she reminded herself, and made a conscious effort to breathe normally. It didn't work, though, and she broke down crying once more, hoping for some help and receiving no sign of any.

* * * *

Time passed. At the window, she saw Blaron's men patrolling outside, guns at the ready. Karen couldn't tell how much air she had left, but in the back of her mind, she felt that she only had a few minutes. In those minutes, she wondered if anyone on Earth would miss her. Alone and abandoned, she reasoned that only Ron would wonder at her disappearance. No one else would bother. They had their own lives.

She desperately wished for someone — anyone — to come along, but it seemed as though her luck had run out. With a sigh, bereft of hope, she sat on the ground and fought the urge to rip off her breather and end it all right here and now.

"Stop them!" she heard someone shout.

What was...?

The sound of an explosion startled her. Another explosion, this one nearer to her position, caused the ground to heave and toss her from the chair. Getting unsteadily to her feet, she looked out the window and a cloud of smoke billowed over the entire area, making it difficult to see. "Leave them. Leave them!" she heard one of the pig men shout.

Leave what?

As Karen scoped out the area, the smoke cleared and she saw that Blaron's men were no longer around. Taking a chance, she stepped outside and found the night lit up by fire. Clodda's people ran by her, firing their metallic weapons and shouting vicious epithets at a group of people off to her right. In the firelight, she saw other beings running in different directions.

One of them ran at her with a large, curved sword held high in a hand the size of a catcher's mitt. At well over seven feet in height, it moved very quickly, and its face was that of an eel with slanted, evil-looking eyes and a triple-headed tongue that flicked itself in her direction. The sword descended and it was blocked by one of the Narrians. The sword fell from the eel man's hand, and the Narrian snatched it in mid-air and used it to dispatch his foe.

It fell to the ground noiselessly. To see someone killed so quickly with a slash that cut it in half repulsed her, but at the same time, this situation was real and it was dangerous. She had no other choice but to get used to it. "Thanks," she managed to get out.

"You are welcome," he answered, his breath coming out in sharp pants. "I saw you emerge from our building and came to help." He gave a sharp whistle and another man ran up, carrying the snake cages.

"What's going on?" she asked.

The first man spoke, still breathing hard. "A rival group of poachers has arrived. They are fighting with the first group we encountered," he answered, his eyes wild with the heat of battle. "And we are fighting both groups." Twisting his head left and right, he looked around and grabbed her hand. "Come with us."

Both men led her hurriedly to the path from which she'd come. Explosions went off from a few yards away, and Karen lost her balance more than once. The leader grabbed her shoulder the second time she fell and urged her forward. "Hurry," he said. "We must hurry."

Another bomb went off. Whoever was shooting had good aim, as the explosions were getting closer. They whistled through the air and threw up chunks of hard rock and pebbles that clattered off her mask. It was darker than before, and with the smoke from the battle and the noise, it was difficult for her to get her bearings. "Which way is it?" she asked, confused.

The leader's strong hand grasped her arm and he hauled her along until she saw a break in the rock formation. He pointed dead ahead. "Your vessel is over there. Go straight and you shall find it. Here. These are yours, now." He took the cages from the other man and shoved them at her. She clutched them to her breast. "Take good care of them."

Before she could get a word of thanks in, they ran off. Karen started to limp-jog as fast as her legs could carry her. A few steps down the path, she felt a catch in her throat and knew that time was short. Too bad that this breather didn't have some kind of timer to tell her how many minutes she had left.

Holding her breath, she continued on in the direction of the ship, clutching the cages to her chest. She'd gotten halfway there when Blaron's voice rang out behind her. "You are indeed fortunate, Karen Fox. Let us see how fortune favors you now!"

Pivoting around, she saw him raise a long, slender tube to his shoulder. He wore an evil smile and waved goodbye. Just before he fired, a small, round object landed near him and he gave a cry of surprise. It went off with a loud bang and he screamed in pain.

"How did you like that?" she yelled. Her right leg hurt, but the ship was in sight and she started to run once again.

Over the sounds of explosions she heard a different one, like a loud squeak, and she doubled her speed. A millisecond later, something hit her in the back and she felt pebbles strike her arms and shoulders. Her legs gave out under her and she sprawled on the ground, the cages flying out of her hands.

"He shot me," she groaned, and turning over, examined her body all over. Expecting to find blood on her arms or legs, she saw nothing, and in a state of semi-panic now, got to her feet, grabbed the cages and started moving again.

"Almost there," she puffed, and shut her mouth, breathing as shallowly as possible. If anyone was following her, they were doing a good job of keeping silent. Right now, though, she didn't care. The ship loomed in the darkness, the gangplank down and the door open.

A hissing sound got her attention. The air tube attached to her breather had been damaged. Blaron had good aim. Oxygen was escaping, and with it, her life. She gasped and held her breath.

The ship lay ahead, now perhaps a hundred feet away. It might as well have been a thousand as her lungs failed her. Karen stumbled and fell for the second time and the impact of hitting the ground knocked out whatever breath was left in her lungs.

A spasm ran through her body when she breathed in the toxic air. Her body began to shake uncontrollably and her vision grew black. *Oh God, this is it.*

With what she thought was her final breath, she fumbled with the locks of the cages, attempting to free the snakes, but had no strength left. Hands numb, the cages fell from her grasp. *Let them out... Let them escape.*

With a last valiant effort, she managed to raise her arm a few inches, then her strength left her and more toxic fumes entered her lungs. The shaking continued and she figured Blaron would be happy that he got his revenge. *This is it... This is...how it has to be...*

A hand came out of nowhere and grabbed on to her shoulder. She felt her body being dragged through the grass, up the gangplank and onto the ship. Once lying on the hard metal, she lost consciousness and hoped that death would be kind to her.

Chapter Nine
Birthday

"How are you?" a voice asked.

Karen blinked and opened her eyes. Her hands felt a blanket on top of her and she pushed it down. Where was—

Oh wait, she was alive after all. She remembered the explosions, the shouting and the ugly face of Blaron as he waved goodbye. She remembered running to the ship, her oxygen supply exhausted, and the scorching of her lungs as she inhaled Delberon's toxic atmosphere. Then all she saw was blackness and now...

This had to be the infirmary. She recognized the panels in the wall. Comfortable cushions were tucked under her head, and when she pulled the blanket off, she saw that someone had dressed her in a kind of off-white button-down hospital gown. With a grunt, she levered herself up into a sitting position. "How are you?" the voice came again.

"I feel like hammered garbage." A cough erupted from her lungs and it hurt, as if a fire had been built inside her and wanted out. She also felt incredibly weak. Once the coughing fit subsided, she twisted her head around to see who'd asked the question and found Ralus standing just a few feet away, a solemn look on her face.

"Hey, what happened?" Karen asked. Her voice sounded weak to her ears, and her throat hurt. A glass of clear liquid sat near her, and carefully picking it up and taste-testing it, it turned out to be water. She took a sip and set it down. "What happened?"

Ralus' face had worry lines etched in her forehead. "You've been sleeping for two days," she said, her voice shaky. "We brought you here as soon as we could."

Had she been out that long? "Two days..." Karen managed to say. "I've been out two days?"

"I came out to get you when you fell down, but I couldn't get you right away. The poachers were shooting, and we had to wait until the ship's guns fired at them." Ralus crossed her arms over her skinny chest. "The little creature...the tolop got you."

Karen's eyes bugged out. "It did? But the air was...poisonous. It could have died." She looked around, but the creature was nowhere to be seen. It was probably wandering around the ship.

"You were out there," Ralus repeated. "The air didn't bother it." She offered a brief shrug. "It's got a different kind of body, I guess. Once it got you inside, the ship took off and I dragged you here and changed your clothes for you." An accusatory look appeared on her face. "You're a lot heavier than you look."

Guider appeared with its usual popping sound. "We are glad to see that you are awake and well, Karen. Our medical scanners show that while your bodily systems are weak, you have suffered no lasting effects from being exposed to Nar's atmosphere. We hope that you have thanked your rescuers."

A sudden constriction in Karen's chest caused her to cough. After clearing her throat, she said, "Yeah, I was just doing that. Everything's sort of a blur, though."

"We will show you."

Guider threw up a video, taken from the perspective of the ship. It showed the poachers firing at the ship, the ship's stun guns returning fire, then it cut to a shot of the tolop strutting down the gangplank then sprinting on two of its tentacles with a surprising burst of speed over to her position. Reaching out with one of its tentacles, it then hauled her back to the ship with little effort.

The video finished with the tolop running out yet again to retrieve both cages. It came back long enough to deposit them on the gangplank. The video abruptly cut out after the final image. "The hebiran are safe in their enclosure," Guider said.

During the instant replay, Ralus remained silent. Karen, thoroughly touched by the tolop's courage, slowly got to her feet, stood unsteadily for a moment then got her balance back. Once ready, she hugged Ralus and whispered, "Thanks for bringing me here, and when I see the little guy, I'll thank him — or it, too. You've some steel in you."

"Is that a good thing?" Ralus asked in a tentative manner.

"Yeah, it is."

Karen turned around and asked Guider, "Where are we?"

In answer, a holographic map appeared, showing their position in the star system. The details showed a tiny ball speeding past a star cluster, and she figured that it had to be the ship. Guider confirmed it.

"This is us. We were fortunate that a rival group of poachers showed up at approximately the same time Blaron's men did. Our sensors show that they are still fighting with each other on Nar, and that the Narrians are fighting them."

"At least that'll keep all three sides busy for a while," she said. What had Blaron yelled out, something about luck? Right now, she certainly felt that she had to be the luckiest person alive.

"We think it will," Guider answered. "At any rate, we are taking a different route back to our world as the poachers most certainly know our destination. Once they stop fighting with each other, though, they will come after us. Our route is circuitous, to be sure, and although it will take a little longer, it is necessary."

They knew where the final destination was. A shudder of fear ran through her. "But if they know where we're going, won't they be waiting for us? I mean, I remember you have planetary defenses and all that, but what if they get us before we reach your planet?"

"It is a risk that we shall have to take. Although we are cloaked from their sensors, we cannot stay hidden forever. Sooner or later, the strain will be too much for our engine systems to handle."

"I thought you said that your power source was strong," Karen pointed out, turning over all the possibilities in her mind and coming up with nothing.

The answer came quickly. "We thought so as well, but the latest incidents, the cumulative systemic damage and the fact that the cloaking system uses three times as much power than is the norm has all combined to drain our systems. We are on limited power as of this moment."

Karen walked a few paces, tested her legs and found that she wasn't any worse off than when she'd first come aboard. "So...what do we do now?"

"If you are well enough to work, there is a schedule to be kept. Ralus has been doing your work for you —"

"And I'm not so good at it," Ralus interrupted, good mood gone now. Her lower lip curled into an adolescent pout. "Karen's better...the animals like her more."

Gratified though she was at the compliment, Karen had other things on her mind. "How long will it take to get...wherever we're going?"

"On our current course, we will reach our destination in approximately five days."

If ever there was a time to prove oneself, this was it. Karen's body ached and her breathing still wasn't all there...but she had a job to do.

"I'm ready," she said. "I can do it, and" — she stole a look at Ralus — "I've got my assistant with me."

At her pronouncement, Ralus' bad mood vanished and her mouth split into a wide grin. "Then I am part of a team."

* * * *

Once back to her routine, Karen found a measure of comfort doing her daily duties, and all the animals that were oxygen breathers came out of their enclosures to meet her. Only the Malurian dragon and its mate stayed inside, but the male came close enough to the exit in order to give her its usual head-nudge.

The female, Karen noticed, had numerous teats, large, like a cow's, and they seemed to be engorged, as if ready to be suckled at any moment. She went over the file on the dragon, but there wasn't much on the birth part, aside from the basic information that it often gave birth in the wild. She decided to leave it alone. It needed time to rest.

As for the other animals, they let out a chorus of cries, hoots, squeals and other noises that could only be found in the realms of the alien and truly weird. While they couldn't talk, they did make more noise around her than usual, and she figured that it was their way of communicating.

"Yeah, you missed me," she said. "God, I was gone just a couple of days and it's like a camp reunion or something."

Feeding time at the zoo, and at the canarians' enclosure, the birds swooped down to meet her and waited patiently while she walked over to the feed lever. Seeds tumbled out and the canarians pecked away then flew up to settle on her shoulders and rub their massive beaks against her helmet.

After exiting the enclosure, Karen found Ralus waiting by the door, her arms folded. "They still like you a lot better, and you know it. I have to clean the other enclosures."

However, the expression on her face was far from sour. She actually seemed pleased, and before walking away, asked, "Can we go flying later on?"

Flying, she means with the actillions. In truth, Karen was secretly looking forward to taking a ride. "Yeah, we're on. Let's wait a couple of hours."

Ralus disappeared inside one enclosure, and Karen stole a look at Guider as it hovered nearby. With a sudden shock that wasn't really one, she realized that the Keepmasters had seen everything, yet said nothing to her about letting the animals out before. But that was then and this was now. *Oh crap...this could mean trouble.*

Guider abruptly vanished. However, it was a sure bet that sooner or later the Keepmasters were going to question the decision to let the animals roam free, so once the morning chores were over and Ralus had passed out in their room, Karen went up to the bridge in order to get some answers.

As a preamble, she asked, "What's going to happen to the animals once they're on your planet?"

The stars winked out their eternal light at her, but Karen paid them no attention. She kept her eyes focused on the floating metal ball that served as her guide and interpreter.

"They will enter enclosures similar to these," Guider said. "It is doubtful, though, that they will roam free as you have let them." Its voice sounded only mildly disapproving.

So much for segueing into the topic she wanted to talk about, Karen thought. "You've been watching me, er...us?"

"We have. While there were other, more important duties to attend to during the previous crises, our ship has hidden cameras inside every enclosure and all over the park area and they are watching what goes on at every moment of every day. This is for safety reasons as well as security ones."

It pissed Karen off to know that she'd been spied on, but all the same, this was their ship and they could see what they liked. "I can explain—" she started to say.

"Let us explain for you."

Guider threw up a screen and a video replay showed her and Ralus riding the dragon, flying with the moths and enjoying time with another member of the menagerie, a ten-limbed being called a witta, something the size of a human dwarf with a gray shell. Much like a pill bug, it had the ability to roll up into a ball and it enjoyed being kicked and tossed. Guider shut off the instant replay. "I imagine that you have something to say, as opposed to engaging in, shall we say, ball games with animals?"

"Well, yeah, I do," Karen said, thinking about how things were on Earth. "On my world, we have open zoos, a lot like this one. The animals don't know each other, so we have glass screens. But they can still walk around."

She bit her lip. "I don't know that much about these animals, but I wanted them to have a little freedom," she answered while carefully thinking which words would be appropriate. "I don't think I'd like living in a cage all the time, either. They seem tame enough."

"This is a controlled environment," the answer came. "And while the animals are somewhat domesticated, they may not exhibit the same level of openness with anyone else. Caution is still advised, no matter how friendly you think they are."

Its response only answered part of her question. "All right, I'll be careful. So what's going to happen to them? How long will they spend on your world?"

Guide meditated on her question for a while, bobbing up and down. "Everything depends on a number of factors—how long it will take the other worlds to rebuild their ecological systems, how long it will take for the animals to produce sufficient numbers of offspring to allow the species to escape its endangered status. There are an infinite number of factors, and they are all malleable at this point. Our best estimation would be five to ten years, by your Earth standards.

"Additionally, as these animals have lost their instincts for the most part, they can never return to their home environments. They have had a relatively easy life in the time they've spent on this ship. To send them back to their own worlds would be a death sentence for them."

Wait a minute. "Don't the people from the planets have any say?"

"Explain yourself." The voice came out impersonally, but with an edge of iron to it. Obviously, the Keepmasters knew everything, but it seemed as though they wanted to test her recently learned knowledge.

Karen worried her lower lip between her teeth as she searched for the correct words. "I'm not an expert, but I remember that the actillion can reproduce in any environment and doesn't need to worry about where it lives. And the faderum... they like being in groups, not just pairs. The only reason you've got them is to breed them, right?"

"Correct."

Putting her thoughts together, she pressed her point. "What I'm saying is, you're protecting them, but you're taking away what they are. They're supposed to be in the wild. I think that if you save them on your world, then once the other worlds are back to normal, you could—"

"We have tried that," Guider interrupted, and this time its voice sounded weary. "At the beginning, we did as you suggested. We rescued them and then waited until the wars ceased on their planets. However, these animals are not the same as the ones that perhaps you are used to on Earth. Once out of their environment for even a short time, they forget how to interact and how to survive. They would not live for very long back home.

"However, if they could go back with their offspring, they might have a better chance. This is also what we've found. Please believe us when we say that we are not heartless. What we do is for the animals' own wellbeing. The leaders of the various worlds we have dealt with also agree with our decision."

Guider's answer made sense, so Karen turned the conversation in a different direction. "Tell me about Ralus," she continued. "What's going to happen to her?" When no answer came her way, she repeated, "What's going to happen? She's got a life, too."

There was still no reply, so finally she tapped the metal ball with her finger. "Are you going to answer me or what?"

"What would you have us do?"

Say what? Karen's jaw dropped open. "You're going to give these animals a home, but you're not going to give a person a place to live?" Angry tears started from her eyes. "What kind of people are you?"

"We did not say that we would not accept her," Guider replied in a level tone. "We simply asked you what you would do."

Hastily wiping her eyes, Karen blurted out, "I'd take her back to Earth with me. She, uh, could live there."

"You would do that, knowing what her appearance is and how it differs from the appearance of your people. When on your world, we did not have sufficient time in order to thoroughly access your records. However, we did find many instances of crimes committed against those of color or different races than what is considered the norm."

Karen fell silent. Why argue with the metal ball? She'd never had a problem with anyone else's color or religion, but only an idiot would say that the Earth was perfect. Being rejected was something she knew all too well.

"And what would the authorities on your world say?" Guider continued. "More specifically" — it flew down to meet her at eye level — "what would they do?"

Karen didn't have to answer. Ralus was an alien. She'd be arrested, taken into custody, studied, and her life would be over. She was only thirteen or so, but on Earth, the people would never understand. Instinctively, her hand reached up to touch her scar.

"All right, you win," she muttered, sour that the conversation had come to this. "What *are* you going to do?"

Guider pulled back a few inches. "As we know our solar system slightly better than you do, we are in contact with a number of compatible worlds. Once our animals have been properly settled, we will make arrangements."

Karen sighed...then grew suspicious. "If you were going to do all that, why did you ask me in the first place?"

Guider didn't answer, so Karen grabbed the little ball and held it an inch away from her mouth. "Tell me!"

"We were not sure that your intentions were honest. You have complained much in the short time you have been here."

With a sudden cry of rage, Karen hurled Guider from her. It struck the side of the wall and rebounded off it, spinning wildly in the air. "Hey, you kidnapped me!"

she spit out. "*You* kidnapped *me*. You took me from my planet and forced me to work up here. I didn't have a choice. And I think that I've done my job just fine. So don't talk to me about honest intentions when you're just full of lies!"

Guider remained silent, and Karen's ire spilled over. "You said that this ship was on some sort of preset course, that you had to stay on the flight plan, right? I remember. But then we went to Delberon to pick up the snakes. So you lied to me then, too, didn't you?"

"Yes…we did."

"Oooooh!" she screamed, and if she'd had the ability to launch a spinning kick a la Chuck Norris, she would have done it. "You've been…been BS-ing me all this time, so why should I bother listening to you now?"

"We ask of you that you do this as you are the only one who can."

That answer was no answer at all, and swearing at the top of her lungs, Karen stalked off the bridge and went back to her room, only to find Ralus up and playing solitaire. "I am winning at this game, too," Ralus said.

Her manner was so innocent that Karen decided against continuing her mad-on at the Keepmasters. What was the use? After blowing out a deep breath, she offered a brief smile. "I think I taught you too well," she stated.

"It is a fun game," Ralus answered as she laid down the last of the cards. "It's fun for me."

Her answer made Karen laugh and her bad mood vanished. After sitting down to massage her bad leg, she said, "So, I have a question. Where do you want to live when this is all over?"

Ralus' good humor vanished and she put the cards down. "I don't know. Anywhere is okay if I can have friends. I don't need much." The corners of her mouth twisted upward in a smile. "Can we play some gin rummy?"

"Sure."

As Ralus dealt, Karen wondered what would really happen then decided not to think about it too much. She had three jacks, two queens and a lot of low-count cards. This was one game she did not want to lose.

* * * *

The next morning, Karen had just finished feeding the canarians when she heard Ralus screaming her name. She made her way over as fast as possible and found her in front of the Malurian dragons' enclosure. She was pacing back and forth and running her hands nervously over her head as if having the mother of all panic attacks. "What's going on?"

"I walked in to clean up and the female was groaning and twitching," Ralus blurted out, on the verge of tears. "I didn't know what to do, so I called you."

Going over to the dragon's side, Karen knelt down and ran her hand along the abdomen. The baby inside had kicked her before, but now it seemed as if the legs were powerful enough to split the skin. This was not good.

The male came over and grunted, its head swinging back and forth. In order to have some quiet, Karen put a pair of sunglasses on it and asked Ralus to take it outside. "Take him for a walk. I'll take care of the mother."

Consulting her pocket guide to interstellar life, she found nothing of value. It simply stated that the Malurian dragons were used to giving birth under incredibly difficult conditions. On their world, they could exist in deep snow, extremely dry and arid temperatures and high altitudes... The list went on. And since they'd been giving birth for millennia, what did they need her for?

Still, Karen couldn't shake the bad feeling and asked Guider to run a more in-depth scan. "Allow us a moment," it said, and she heard a whirring sound as the little ball was probably poring through its memory banks. "The birth is imminent," Guider stated with a note of alarm in its voice.

Karen had heard that note once before when the poachers attacked the ship, but this? The dragon was going to give birth *now*? Its body started to shake, and it subsequently turned all colors of the rainbow, one after the other. Karen had never seen that before, but then again, she was in outer space. Anything and everything probably happened here, including imitating a chameleon. "Oh holy crap...what am I supposed to do?"

"Help her."

Thinking fast, Karen punched the wall panel and thought about a bucket full of water. Doctors always washed their hands first. It appeared and she washed her hands and waited. The female continued to have contractions, and Karen timed them at coming every thirty seconds. What she wouldn't have given for a trained vet to be here right now.

A few seconds later, the female dragon gave out a loud snort followed by a groan. A splash of water then a torrent, poured from her lower regions. She was going to give birth any second. Her lower legs spasmed then stretched straight out, her stomach contracted, and…she stopped. She was still breathing, though, but very erratically.

"What's going on?" Karen asked Guider.

"She is having some difficulty."

Karen almost had a hemorrhage at that comment and exploded with, "Yeah, like tell me something I *don't* know! What kind of trouble is it?"

Guider hovered over the mother dragon's lower body. "It is a breech birth."

The baby was stuck in the opposite position instead of coming out head first. *Marvelous, this would happen.* It would either choke or get its neck snapped. Searching around for something sharp, she found nothing, so she mentally wished for a knife from the ship and one dropped out in a second.

Stealing a look outside, Ralus was still on top of the male, running around the compound. Holding her breath, Karen dipped the knife in the water and made a one-inch cut to the top and bottom of the female's vagina. The female groaned, but stayed still, and blood, greenish-blue, along with a lot of dark fluid poured out and formed a river on the floor.

"Oh hell," Karen whispered, and the female followed up her groan with a bellow in an incredibly loud voice, something that sounded like a foghorn and a boar mating.

A roar sounded from outside, and the male charged in, Ralus hanging on for dear life from its back. It stopped abruptly and Ralus went flying over its head to skid on the floor and land up against the far wall. She hung off the ground, upside down, and then sagged to the hard surface.

"I'm all right," she called.

"Thanks for telling me," Karen murmured, thinking only of the female dragon in front of her. A loud snort made her look up, and the male dragon stood there, swinging his head back and forth, steam and snot erupting from its nostrils. "I'm on it," she said, and wondered why she bothered saying anything to begin with.

With time running out, she had to work and to work fast. Reaching inside with both hands, she encountered thick liquid. "Eeew...oh crap, this is just gross," she breathed.

She got hold of the baby, cupped one hand under its neck and the other under its back, and gently pulled. "C'mon, mom, push!" she urged.

The mother dragon gave one long, continuous bellow and expelled a mass of fluids along with the baby. The bellow then trailed off to a series of soft groans, but the mother looked happier and more relaxed. Her stomach immediately deflated and a sudden rush of liquid came from her opening and covered Karen in slime.

Wiping the water and amniotic fluid away from her face, Karen then cleaned off the baby's body of as much excess gunk as she could and then put it down. It was almost two feet long and weighed a lot. The mother got to her feet and nudged it, but it didn't move. She nudged it again, and it remained unresponsive.

"What's wrong?" Ralus asked.

Karen put her head to the baby's mouth. "It's not breathing."

Guider chose that moment to disappear. The male continued to snort and paw the ground, but stayed in its spot. Karen glanced at it then back at the baby. She put her forefinger and her middle finger into the baby's mouth and down its throat. "Maybe it swallowed the water," she muttered.

The mother gave another heave, and more fluids came out. No placenta. How a baby could be born without one seemed impossible, but Karen realized that she'd already entered into the realm of the impossible. She gently shoved her finger farther down the baby's throat. A second later, the baby gave a huge hiccup and some water trickled out. Karen put her head to the baby's chest. There was a heartbeat, faint and unsteady...then it stopped.

With both hands, Karen pressed gently on the creature's chest. Ralus came over and asked, "What are you doing?"

"It's CPR," Karen answered. "We had to take classes in this at school." And she continued to work. Up, down, up, down and repeat and all the while, the male's snorting got heavier and deeper. Karen worked frantically to get the baby's pump going, and after a minute of pressing on the baby's chest, it suddenly heaved. The animal's eyes opened, it coughed out more water and began to breathe on its own.

Immediately, the male stopped snorting and ambled over to nudge the baby with its snout. The mother began to lick her child all over, cleaning off the excess bodily fluids and waste with her thick tongue. Once cleaned off, the baby gave a sharp trumpeting bleat of its own then moved underneath the mother to start feeding.

With a sigh, Karen sat back tiredly, covered in slime and blood. A sense of accomplishment filled her. She took the opportunity to motion to Ralus to leave the enclosure. The Malurian dragons had to celebrate in their own way.

The door closed behind Karen as she walked outside. Ralus, eyes wide with admiration, said, "That was great! I've never seen anything like that before."

Karen was still shaking the dragon's fluids from her body. "I never want to see anything like that again."

* * * *

Upstairs in her room, she quickly stripped off her uniform and took a long, hot shower, feeling the water blast every speck of dirt and slime from her body. When she came out, she slipped on a new uniform and then noticed that Ralus had already passed out.

After she'd sat down and sipped from a cup of orange juice she'd ordered from the ship's dispensary, Guider popped in. "Hey, nice of you to show up now," Karen said, and didn't bother keeping the sarcasm out of her voice. "Where'd you go before?"

"Our files on the birthing sequences are incomplete," Guider said. "It was necessary to upgrade them. You have done well, Karen."

She felt a tired smile forming at the edges of her mouth and breathed a sigh of relief. "How's mama?"

"See for yourself."

The little orb threw up a video of the newest arrival. It looked like a tiny version of the father and was already nosing around. Karen couldn't tell for sure, but she thought she detected a look of pride on the mother's face. "Well, they seem happy," she said.

"You have done well," Guider repeated. "Perhaps taking you along with us was indeed the wisest choice."

It disappeared and Karen lay down with her hands behind her head, staring at the ceiling. She was exhausted and wanted nothing more than to sleep, but the image of mama, papa and baby wouldn't leave. "Happy birthday," she whispered, satisfied at a job done well. "Have a good one."

Chapter Ten
Find me!

Space was one long continuum, and with nothing in the way of entertainment save the card games—which she always lost. Guider appeared promptly at five in the morning for the next two days to inform her that she had to carry out her duties.

"We are still taking a circuitous route home," Guider said on the third day after the Malurian dragons' baby had been born. "Our sensors show that the poachers' ships are still out there. Forgive us for the inconvenience."

"That's okay," she answered. "I've got work to do."

Guider disappeared and Karen nudged Ralus, who was still sleeping soundly. "Hey, get up. It's feeding time at the zoo."

Ralus awoke in a second and grinned. "When we're done, can we have a race?"

"You're on."

After feeding the canarians, Karen went to check on the Malurian dragons and was astonished to see the baby already trotting around. It had gotten its space legs and it ran around sniffing at every little thing, intensely curious about the goings-on. When Karen walked in to feed its parents, it came over without hesitation, sniffing and giving out baby snorts.

She cautiously put out her hand, and the baby licked it. Its tongue, rough and raspy, scored her flesh, but only in a most pleasant way. Exploration over, it returned to its mother's feeding stations for a drink.

While Karen wanted to play with it, Guider cautioned her not to, not that she needed the warning. "Mothers need time to bond with their children," it warned.

If these animals were anything like human mothers or animals on Earth, they wouldn't like to be disturbed, so she darted in just long enough to do a quick hose-down of the place, deliver the food, and leave. The male's eyes followed her every movement, his eyes hooded and watchful, while the female didn't even glance toward her once. The baby made a few noises and shook its head in Karen's direction, but a harsh grunt from the mother dissuaded it from venturing farther.

Two hours later, she'd finished her chores and Ralus met her in the middle of the park, wearing a happy grin. "I'm done feeding the other animals," she announced. "Can we have our race?"

Karen put away her bucket and grinned. "Moths?" she asked.

"I want the male moth."

Karen was fine with the female. It seemed that the male preferred Ralus, anyway, so after they both clambered up on the moth's backs, Karen pointed at the far end of the zoo. "We go there and back five times. Are you ready?"

"Ready!"

"Giddy-up," Karen said, and gently kicked the side of her mount's body.

The moth took off at high speed, and Karen hung on to the fur on her body. The sound of her wings beating was a loud thrum in her ears, and she urged her moth onward. "Let's go!"

Ralus hung tough, though, and at the end of the fifth lap, they landed in a tie. Karen slid off the moth, which fluttered away with her mate, exuding a strong smell of cedar. She watched them go with a slight sense of regret. This mission would soon be over. No more rides.

Ralus must have picked up on the expression on Karen's face, for she said, "You look sad, Karen. Is something wrong?"

Embarrassed at showing her feelings, Karen shook her head. "No, it's all good. I just, uh… Never mind." She looked around for the tolop, though. Unusual, as the little creature liked to stay by her side. "Where's the tolop?

"I don't know," Ralus said. "Can we eat first?"

Suddenly, a sense of worry spread through Karen's mind. The tolop didn't like to go a day without its tummy rub and it had been gone for almost seventy-two hours, so either it was sick or…she didn't want to think about the alternatives. "Let's search the ship."

They started with the tolop's enclosure. It was clean and sterile smelling. *It hasn't been there for some time.*

"It's not here," she said to Ralus. "Let's take a look at the rest of the ship."

They expanded their search and went through the ship level by level. As Guider had told her earlier on, many of the sections were closed and failed to open up under her touch, and at the end of a long and fruitless search, they came up with nothing.

Karen, supremely frustrated, called out, "Guider, have you seen the tolop?"

The metal ball popped in. "I have scanned the entire vessel. The tolop is not on board."

It's not on board? So where was it? A sick feeling formed in the pit of her stomach as she realized that the impossible had just happened. "You didn't leave it on Delberon, did you?"

Silence followed, and Karen finally erupted and flicked Guider with her finger. It gave a tiny beep of surprise, but did not answer. "You did, didn't you?"

"Apparently we did."

Oh, that was just wonderful, and she had the urge to maim something. Right now, anything would do, and Guider looked like the best target. "We have to go back," she stated.

"We cannot, for it would be too dangerous. Our best plan of action is to return to our world with the animals we have. It would be foolish to risk all of them for only one."

This time Karen let loose with a slap and sent the ball into the wall. It didn't appear to be damaged, but the voice coming from it sounded surprised. "Is that a common human trait, to lash out when frustrated?"

"That's a dumb thing to say," Karen answered, incredibly pissed at the question. "You were going to leave Ralus on her world—alone," she pointed out, clenching her fists. "You didn't have to bring me back to the ship on Delberon. The tolop rescued me. It didn't have to. It *wanted* to. The least I can do is to try and find him or her, er…it."

"We will scan the upcoming worlds," Guider replied. "There are seven in our path back to our point of origin and perhaps the poachers have landed there. We warn you, though, that deviating from our course is dangerous."

What wasn't dangerous? "Well, let's do a recount, shall we?" Karen shot back, not deigning to hide her sarcasm. "So far, we've been shot at twice, I've been attacked and I saw people die." The sarcasm then morphed into rage. "*I* almost died. But if your creed," she spat out the word, "means anything to you, then we've got to find the tolop. That's how it stands."

She waited, fists clenching and unclenching. For all she knew, the tolop was already dead, but maybe the poachers could be dealt with…maybe. "Let me know when you find something," she said. Spinning around on the ball of her good foot, she strode off and made her way back to her room.

"What did you find out?" Ralus asked, once she entered.

"That the Keepmasters don't like keeping their promises," she snarled, kicking the wall. For a moment she forgot that she'd used her bad leg and it sent a shaft of pain up to the crown of her head.

"Damn it," she muttered. "Doing the right thing hurts."

* * * *

Playing cards calmed her down, and losing didn't bother her as much as it used to. She did wonder, though, how Ralus managed to do it. It wasn't like she could see through objects or read someone else's mind. So what was her secret?

Finally, Karen asked, "How is it you're winning all the time? I mean, I don't really mind losing, but you didn't mark the deck, did you?"

"I don't understand," Ralus answered. A guilt-free expression was written all over her face. "I am just playing cards. There are only four types in each suit, just like you taught me, and—"

"You're counting cards!" *Call this a shake-my-head moment.* Karen had heard of some people who had that ability, but she'd never been able to do it. She pointed to the discarded cards that lay in a messy pile. "Tell me the numbers and the suits there."

Ralus promptly replied, "There are twenty-three cards there, six clubs, numbers one, three, seven, jack, queen and ace. Hearts, there are—"

"I get it," Karen interrupted. She had a hand of three hearts and four spades. She put them face down, picked up the rest of the deck, and showed it quickly to Ralus, fanning it out for her benefit. "See that?" When Ralus nodded, Karen asked, "What's in my hand?"

Ralus proceeded to name the exact cards one by one. As she did so, Karen let out a deep breath and she felt a smile coming over her face. "I wish we were in Las Vegas now. We'd break the bank."

"I don't understand…"

The monkey siren went off, startling Karen. She dropped the cards. "What is it?"

Guider appeared at eye level. "We are being hailed. Please come to the bridge."

"I'm not going," Ralus said, her quiet air suddenly gone, and her voice beginning to tremble. "That…that pig is too scary. I want to stay here."

"No problem," Karen said as she headed out of the door and up to the bridge. Once there, the sight of Blaron on-screen assaulted her eyes.

"It seems you are indeed a fortunate girl," he said, his right eye twitching.

Ralus had said he looked too scary. She'd be more afraid now. The right side of Blaron's face had been horribly burned and the skin hung down like melted wax and was a horrible brownish-pink color. Half his hair had been burned away as well. "You don't seem to be," Karen shot back. "Do I smell fried chicken?"

Apparently he understood the reference, as he ground his teeth together. "You try my patience, girl," he snarled and pointed to his scars. "This is a remnant from the last battle with our foes. Now, I look like you."

His barb hurt, but Karen rejoined with, "Yeah, we're a matched pair. And I'm glad you got what was coming to you." It was a childish comeback, but she had to say something.

Blaron, on the other hand, offered a mean smile. "Girl, if you were here right now, I would make both sides of your face match. However, I will hold my temper as I possess something you would dearly like to be returned." He held up the tolop by one of its tentacles and it gave a terrified bleat.

The sight of the little creature being manhandled set her off. "You are *slime!*" she yelled. "Give it back!"

A harsh chuckle emanated from his half-mouth. "Karen Fox, you are in no position to make demands. However, I am open to an exchange. This creature is worthless to us. However, there are other creatures on your vessel that we desire, and my terms are as such and they are not negotiable. We will go to a planet nearby. It is called Ansar. It is an abandoned planet with an oxygen-nitrogen atmosphere, so you will not need a breather. You will bring the hebiran and we will trade this thing for the snakes. That is a most generous deal, and I suggest that you accept my terms."

His eye continued to twitch, and while it was distracting, it made her think that he wasn't so powerful after all. "Hang on a second," she said. "I have to discuss this with my bosses."

"You have one minute."

Whispering to Guider to put the speaker on mute, it did so. "Tell me about Ansar."

"As Blaron has indicated, Ansar is an abandoned planet. Its populace was evacuated when its inner core became unstable. It is subject to volcanic eruptions, sudden electrical storms and other phenomena. It is not a safe place."

And what was? Blaron was just playing with them. She knew that. She also knew that he had no intention of trading straight-up. He had a powerful warship, wanted nothing more to kill her, and she was stepping into the lion's den. "What are you thinking about, Karen?" Guider asked. "If you are afraid, then we can—"

"No, I'll go," she decided. "I'm afraid, yeah, but I have a plan."

"Please inform us."

She did. It all came down to making one interstellar call, working a little magic and hoping that Blaron was as greedy and stupid as she thought he was. Asking Guider to put the speaker on, she relayed her message. "Okay, we have a deal. But we're going to meet, just you and me. Your men show, I bail. You get nothing."

The corner of the undamaged portion of his mouth twitched upward in a half-smile. Attempt at jollity or not, he was still exceedingly ugly. "I shall agree to your terms. We will meet in one hour. Here are the coordinates."

They flashed on the screen. A moment later, the screen went blank.

"We have the coordinates," Guider said. "Please be careful, Karen."

"I will."

First stop, the storage room, and once inside, she searched for the necessary materials. *Where were they…? There*, she exulted. *They'll do.*

Gathering what she needed, Karen headed back to her room and found Ralus playing cards, as usual. The little girl put down the hand she was holding, though, once the door opened, and Karen briefed her on all that had happened and her plan.

"Do you want me to go with you?" she asked.

"No, you're staying here this time," Karen answered. "But if something goes wrong" — she hesitated and took in a deep breath — "if something happens to me, then you take over and get the animals home. You got that?"

In a quick move, Ralus arose and threw her arms around Karen's waist, hugging her tightly. "Don't go," she begged, tears running down the sides of her face. "That man…he isn't a man. He's a monster."

Karen knew that. She was also scared — pee-her-panties, knees-shaking scared — but she couldn't leave the tolop, not after it had helped her. "I have an idea," she said. "And we need to get some cages from the zoo."

Ralus lifted her tear-stained face. "I don't understand."

Karen gently disengaged Ralus' arms from her waist and nodded at the exit. "Come with me. I'll explain on the way."

* * * *

One hour later, the ship touched down at the prescribed coordinates. Ansar was, as Blaron had said, an abandoned world. It was dusk when they arrived, and with a gray sky rapidly turning black and lit by occasional sheets of lightning, it was hard for her to get her bearings at first. Additionally, the heavens pealed with continuous thunder, almost as if some god or gods had grown exceedingly angry with their creation.

She inhaled and immediately coughed. The thin air was breathable, but it held a fine mist of dirt, which made breathing difficult. The ground, dry and brown and cracked, shook almost continuously, and she almost lost her balance as she stepped off the gangplank.

No wonder that this planet had been abandoned. In the distance, numerous volcanoes dotted the landscape. Closer to her position, large cracks in the ground allowed geysers of water to spurt out, and when a few of the drops touched her, she yelped. The water was boiling hot. "Great, more marks," she muttered while looking around. "Why did I come here and where is pig-man?"

A roar of an engine interrupted her thoughts. In the distance, a sleek ship approached. Roughly the size of a jet fighter, it had numerous turrets on its wings. They had to be cannons, she figured. It soared over her position, hung a sharp left and landed about three hundred feet from her position, using a kind of vertical jet. No runway needed for this thing.

Blaron's voice emanated from the craft. "Girl, do you have what I want?"

It appeared that Blaron wasn't the type to exchange pleasantries. She wasn't interested in them, anyway. "I have what you want," she yelled back and felt ridiculous for employing such an overused cliché. Between the sound of thunder and the eruptions from the geysers, she could barely hear her own voice. "Show me the tolop!"

Apparently, Blaron had some kind of high-powered listening device on board his craft, as he immediately replied, "Bring what I have asked for over first. I will meet you halfway. That is the fairest thing to do."

Karen pointed to her ship. "They're in the cargo bay. Wait a minute."

She went up the gangplank, retrieved the glass cages, and walked down to the ground again, striving to keep her balance under the ever-shifting landscape. Blaron's ship's doors opened and he jumped out onto the surface. His wide feet gave him the advantage of sure footing and he strolled toward her in an unconcerned manner. In one meaty hand he held a cage, and once they got close enough, Karen saw the tolop inside, bleating pitifully.

Blaron stopped in his tracks about fifty feet away. He didn't seem to be carrying any weapons, but even so, hand-to-hand she knew that she'd lose. Blaron seemed to know that and wore a smirk on his scarred face. The right side of his face, scarred and ugly, stood out. His right eye and right cheek twitched as if it had suffered nerve damage and he held out the cage. "This is an awful world. Do you know its history?"

"No."

He set the cage on the ground. "Ansar was a mining planet only a decade ago. Its ore was prized among many worlds in this galaxy. It held riches beyond compare. However, when they dug too deeply into the mantle of their planet, their equipment somehow disturbed the core and it became unstable. It produced what you see here." Blaron swept his hand around the desolated landscape. "Those survivors emigrated to another planet elsewhere in this galaxy. And now we stand here, about to trade. You will give me the hebiran and I will give you this worthless creature."

It seemed fair enough, but Karen wondered about something. She'd had her suspicions before, but wanted to make sure. "Do you know anything about the animals you steal?"

He shrugged his massive shoulders. "We know enough to keep them alive until their buyers pay us. Our job does not require us to be experts."

Good enough for her. Karen stepped forward with a smile. "Then you know that being in contact with the tolop can be dangerous if you haven't had your shot."

Blaron's eye twitched. "What are you talking about?"

"It carries the rubella virus," she answered, keeping a straight face and hoping that he was as dumb as he looked. "You did have your shot, right?"

Now a look of alarm formed on Blaron's ugly mug. "What is this virus that you speak of?"

Good, the lie had taken hold, and Karen felt comfortable enough to carry it through. "Oh, you *didn't* have your shot. That's really bad." She set down the cages and folded her arms across her chest. "Well, the virus doesn't show up immediately. It takes about three days for the symptoms to present. You start getting a dry mouth, itchy skin, and red spots break out all over your face. There are two types, the red and the black. The black ones are the worst."

Another twitch came from his eye. "Describe more of the symptoms to me."

Thinking fast, she added, "I'm not an expert, but from what I know, you start to feel bad all over, then you start itching really bad, and…" She spread her arms wide.

"Then what?" he demanded.

"Then you die."

What Karen had just described was the Earth variety of measles, but she knew that Blaron probably knew nothing about her world, much less its diseases. And he was more than likely ignorant of the other species he and his men carried.

Now Blaron's body started to quiver and his right eye twitched in a mad dance. "Girl, if you are lying to me —"

"I've already had my shots," she answered in a blithe tone. "I'm immune. Check with your ship if you don't believe me."

A sudden movement under her feet caused her to stumble. After she regained her balance, she saw Blaron talking into a small box the size of a television's remote control. It had to be a communicator. He closed it and shoved it in his pocket. "I have relayed the information to my men. They are checking now and will be here shortly."

It figured he'd try and pull something like this.

"Hey, we had a deal," she said and stabbed her finger at the ground. "You come alone and I come alone. That's what you said. What kind of crap is this?"

He pointed at the ship behind her. "Your vessel is there. You have a means of escape from this cursed world. My main vessel is in orbit fifty thousand kilometers from this position. What you see before you is my scout ship. I have upheld my end of the bargain. We shall exchange cages and then I shall leave. You are lucky that I am not armed or else I would have already killed you by now. I have not forgotten about my brother."

A murderous spark flared in his eyes and Karen knew that he wanted revenge in the worst way. She steeled herself, picked up the cages and walked half the distance between them. "Fine, we'll exchange cages and you can leave. Take your stupid snakes. I don't want them."

Blaron chuckled and picked up the tolop's cage. "They will be compensation for all that you have put me through."

He walked toward her, and at the meeting point, they slowly extended their arms. Karen knew that he didn't trust her. Part one of the plan was already complete. She just had to wait for part two.

There was a moment of hesitancy before the handoff, but the exchange went smoothly, and the tolop mewled when it saw Karen. Blaron's face twisted into a smile as he received his bounty, but then a beep sounded from his communicator. He took it out and opened it. "What is it?"

Karen started to back up ever so slowly as the pirate kept asking "What?"

She'd gotten halfway to her ship when Blaron looked in her direction, his smile now gone and his voice rose with each passing word. "That was my ship. We have searched the interstellar records for rubella. Do you take me for a fool? It is a childhood disease on your world," he bellowed. "For your insolence, I shall break your neck."

The cords on his neck stood out as he spoke and his pale face purpled with rage. "Bring the ship to this position," he roared into his communicator. "Train all weapons on the Keepmasters' vessel!"

"You'd better check on your cargo first," she said and kept edging backward.

Blaron stared at her with a blank look then tore open the cage doors. Two rubber snakes with cheerful little painted smiles on their faces tumbled to the ground. "It's amazing what some rubber hose and a little paint can do," she taunted.

"You will die!" he screamed. "We will kill you, your passenger and you will…"

His words got drowned out by the sight of another vessel coming in hard and fast. This one was differently shaped, cubic and bristling with guns. "Say hi to plan number two," she called out. "These guys want some payback, so if I were you, I'd run."

Blaron looked up in alarm. "We shall meet again," he declared. In spite of his bulk, he did a passable imitation of an Olympic runner as he sprinted to his ship.

Yeah, you run. The ground started to shake violently and she fell hard on her side. "Ow…what's going on?"

A mini-geyser erupted ten feet away, and she threw herself to one side to avoid getting scalded. Less than a second later, the ground started to crack under her feet. This was definitely a double not good moment.

"This has to happen now?" she yelled.

As she got to her feet, more fissures opened up, and the cage tumbled out of her hands, bounced along the surface and fell into one of the cracks. On hands and knees, she followed its path. The palms of her hands and the skin on her knees tore on the sharp rock, but she ignored the pain.

"I'm coming!" she cried.

Two feet away lay a fissure. The tolop bleated and she laboriously made her way over to where she found the cage wedged between two rocks. The ground still trembled and she was afraid the rocks would crash together.

"Hang on!" Karen yelled, and crawled over the side, reaching out for the handle at the top of the cage. She'd almost reached it when another tremor hit and the rocks started to close.

"No!" she screamed, but stopped when she saw the tolop's tentacles shoot out and hold the rock back. In an effortless movement, it kept the rocks from crushing the cage. With a last-ditch effort, she stretched out her arm and snagged the cage. "Gotcha!" her voice rang out in triumph.

Triumph turned to terror as the land under her feet started to disintegrate. "Oh crap," she gasped.

Getting to her feet, she moved toward the ship faster than she initially thought possible. Land fell away behind her in chunks as she awkwardly ran, desperately clutching her cargo. "Guider," she yelled, praying that it was listening, "get ready to leave!"

After Karen reached the ship and throwing herself on board, the orb appeared.

"We have been watching. We are leaving now."

With a click, the doors slammed shut, and the ship took off in a burst of speed. The sudden acceleration threw her against the wall and the tolop bleated in alarm. After getting to her feet, she opened the door of the cage and the creature jumped into her arms and clung to her like a baby. "Yeah, you want your hug," she said, breathing hard. "Let's see what's going on out there."

Up on the main bridge, Karen stared at the screen. Blaron's ship and the other poacher's ship were exchanging shots of some kind of energy plasma. Guider appeared at eye level. "It seems that calling the enemy was a sound battle plan," it said. "They appear to be occupied with each other for the moment."

"Good," Karen decided. "Then I need a shower and my little friend needs a nap."

She made her way back to her quarters and found Ralus already passed out. Awake for the food and asleep for the battle, Karen considered, as fatigue washed over her. She stripped off her uniform after putting the tolop down.

"Wait here," she said, and it sat calmly, clicking its eyes.

The hot water felt good, and when Karen re-entered the room, she got a fresh uniform from the ship's dispenser, slipped it on and said, "Come here."

Every bone and muscle in her body hurt, but the softness of the floor and the warmth of the blanket took some of the pain away. The tolop obediently jumped into her arms and she rubbed its belly. "Don't you ever run off again," she counseled in a mock-scolding tone. "You're staying here with me."

Chapter Eleven
Say farewell

"What will you do after we deliver the animals?" Ralus asked as she laid down another winning hand at gin rummy.

Another loss and I'm beginning to hate this game. Karen looked at her hand of cards with dismay. They'd been playing cards for the last couple of hours in the cabin and her opponent had won every hand. "Just when you think you have the right combo, you don't," she murmured.

Losing sucked, but you couldn't always win, and Karen had other things on her mind. Check on the baby dragon, comb the moths' backs, go for a ride later...and, oh yeah, the question. She leaned back against the wall and sighed. "I don't really know."

That was the million-dollar question she'd been asking herself for the last few days. Job over, what would she do? The Keepmasters said that they'd provide transportation home, but what did she have to go back to? An empty house, more rehab and a dearth of friends in her life…

"Karen."

"What is it?"

Ralus touched her arm, bringing her out of her reverie. She had a look of eagerness on her face. "Can I go with you to your home? I guess that you miss your world."

Did she? Karen estimated that she'd been in space roughly ten days. At first, she'd been somewhat homesick, hating her life here, but now that the journey was almost at an end…

"No, not really," she decided to say.

Ralus plowed ahead, ignoring her answer. "I don't have anyone," she said. "I used to have a place to live. Now" — a note of ineffable sadness entered her voice — "now I don't. If I could stay with you, I could learn about your world."

Learning about Earth…Karen almost snorted with disgust. Learning meant knowing about what was different. Kids learned that very early on in life. Would Ralus like to be treated as a freak? Did she know what would happen? Young kids were innocent. Innocence, though, was easily corrupted and twisted, and if you looked or sounded different, then the world could indeed be a cruel place. No one deserved to be treated like a freak or an object of amusement or hatred.

If there'd been any way to say something positive about living on Earth, Karen would have said it, but she couldn't. At the same time, though, she didn't want to be mean. She'd had enough meanness in her life already. Instead, she put on a smile and said, "You know, it would be cool if the Keepmasters let you. I'm up for it. Or maybe you might like their world."

Ralus' face wore a somber expression as she picked up the cards, riffled through them, then seemed to lose interest and dropped them. "I don't know their world. I knew one — mine. I just want a friend to be around."

Her reply, so simple and naïve and pure, made Karen want to cry. That was all she'd ever wanted as well. Forcing out as jolly an answer as possible, she said, "We'll try to find you somewhere to live."

Ralus' face brightened. Her mood seemed to swing back to the positive side of things, for she picked up the cards and clumsily shuffled them. "Thank you. It's good to have a place to live."

Yeah, tell me about it. Then Karen got up. "I'm going to the bridge. Do you want to come with me?"

"I want to practice some more," Ralus answered, her fingers slowly halving the deck.

"Catch you later."

Up on the bridge, Karen stared out at the stars. "Guider," she called out. "How much longer is this going to take?"

As she stood facing the viewing screen, she somehow felt as if she was in command. It was an idle thought as the ship was automated, but all the same, she felt as though the ship was relying on her to make the big decisions.

As for the stars, they whizzed by, blips of light paving the way ahead in the eternal darkness of space, and she felt impatient as well as somewhat sad that this journey was almost at an end.

"We are approximately one solar day from our home world," Guider said. "We are set now. All the animals seem to be doing well, and we are on course."

"Good to know," Karen offered, still wondering what it would be like where she was landing. A number of other questions ran through her mind, mainly about who'd take care of the animals once things were settled, but a shockwave ran through the ship and threw her to the ground.

Another blast hit and the lights flickered as the monkey siren went off. "Let me guess," she yelled out over the din. "The cloaking isn't working and we've got company?"

"Yes, we do."

The view screen showed Blaron's vessel dead ahead and a lot of lights coming from it. "Can we outrun him?"

"No," the answer came, "but there is an interstellar dust cloud nearby."

Karen thought fast. "Is it like the ice field?"

"What do you mean?"

"I mean can it hide us from their sensors or whatever they have?"

"Yes."

That made the decision easy. "Well, then let's do that," she said and got to her feet. "I'll go check on our other passenger."

Down in her quarters, Karen found Ralus huddled in a ball with the tolop sitting next to her, bleating.

"Hey, I'm here," she said to the younger girl. "It's going to be okay."

As for the tolop, the creature leaped into Karen's arms and she rubbed its stomach until it became calm.

At least someone is calm. She wasn't sure that she could maintain her grip on sanity as the ship continued to rock and the siren continued to wail. Ralus started to sob. Karen sat beside her and put her arms around her shoulders in a gesture designed to impart confidence.

"Hang tough, okay? We're going to make it. Guider's taking the ship to a dust cloud. We can hide there."

As she spoke, she realized how ridiculous it sounded, but in a situation like this, a person had to show some guts. The ship continued to rock and then the lights cut out, plunging the room into darkness. Ralus wailed and Karen hushed her. "Cool it, we're getting through this. We're almost home."

Home was a planet with no name and they were close but yet so far from it. *Take it one quadrant at a time*. The siren continued to sound, Ralus continued to cry, and with a sudden blare, another sound, the sound of engines laboring, came through.

"I don't like the noise I'm hearing," she said. "What is that?"

Guider didn't bother to make its presence known, so Karen grabbed Ralus' hand. "We're going down to engineering," she said. "Stay here, tolop," she ordered, and the little starfish-ray clicked its eyes as if obeying her command. *It will be fine*. Karen got to her feet and pulled Ralus out of the door with her. From there, they took the elevator to the engine room.

Smoke filled the air as she emerged, making her cough. She yelled out, "Guider! Do you have air vents down here?"

A second later, a whooshing sound came through and the smoke disappeared. After Karen got her breath back, Guider popped in, settling near the ceiling. It emitted a yellow light that cut through the smoke. A few seconds later, the light shut off and Guider flew down to hover next to Karen's shoulder. "They are functional now," it said. "They were temporarily damaged in the attack. We are safe for the moment, hidden in the dust cloud."

Interstellar was not on her list of things she knew. "Can you give me a rundown on the cloud, please? I'm not all that great with astronomy."

In answer, another holographic image of space appeared. It showed an immense purplish-black swirling cloud of what appeared to be dust. Bright patches that she thought represented chunks of ice were scattered throughout and they twinkled a greeting. In the center of the projection, Karen spotted a ball-shaped object. "That's us, isn't it?" she asked, pointing to the ball.

"It is," Guider answered. "This is the Majorran Nebula, a dust cloud of immense size. It is well known in this quadrant of space. It is famous for its lights as well as its ability to cloud sensors, as you surmised before. It is very much like the ice field we previously encountered. We have adapted our instruments to overcome this problem. We are not sure about the poachers, though."

Guider's voice sounded uncertain and Karen grew suspicious. "What else aren't you telling me?"

"There is a problem with the engines."

Oh marvelous. What else can go wrong? She then stopped herself from thinking the obvious, as a *lot* could go wrong. In fact, a lot had already gone wrong.

"What's the problem?"

"The conduit which transfers the tranium from the main reactor to the engines has been damaged, thereby stopping the flow of energy to the rokkolufa mechanism, which in turn—"

"I don't speak galactic," Karen interrupted, feeling frustrated at how everything had suddenly gone south. "Is the main engine broken?"

"It is."

Ralus looked like she was going to cry again, and Karen quietly swore. Her parents had always cautioned her to have good manners, but there was a time and a place for everything and this situation demanded a few four-letter words. "All right, the main engine is broken, but do we have alternate engines or sources of power?"

While Guider hummed, Karen fumed, pacing back and forth. How could a ship get broken so fast? She hoped that the people in charge knew how to fix it. Her thoughts of who was at fault here were interrupted by the little machine beeping.

"There is a possibility," Guider intoned. "In the past, we used a power source known as tallonium. We discontinued its use as tranium was more efficient, but our engines can accept it as a viable power source. It will reduce our power, and our shielding will not be at one hundred percent, but it will be sufficient to take us back to our planet, even if our cloaking will not work properly."

When one's hopes were lifted, they dared not hope for too much. Karen knew she shouldn't ask, but since no one else was going to do it...

"Okay, so where do we find this, um, tallonium? Is it radioactive or anything? What does it—?"

"I have accessed the ship's database, and there is a planet fairly close to our location. It is called Larjas Seven," Guider cut in. "It will take another day to reach there, and if we are fortunate, we will be able to find the power source. It is a raw ore that we need, and it is found in the mines of the planet. The rocks are roughly two pounds in weight, as calculated by your Earth's measuring systems."

"What about the people there?"

Instantly, a holographic image sprang up from Guider's body. The inhabitants of the planet looked like crab-shaped beings roughly the size of a toaster. "They are friendly with our planet," Guider said. "The area to which we are going has been temporarily abandoned, and you will find the mine to be empty."

While it sounded simple, plans could be anything but, and suddenly Karen got a very bad feeling. Go to the planet—the ship could do that. Use the ore as an alternate source of power—the ship could do that, too. That left one outstanding question. "And, um, who exactly is going to collect this power source?"

Guider dropped down to meet her eyes. "I am a very small machine, and as was explained before, there are no other robotic devices capable of lifting the ore."

Ralus turned to Karen with a questioning look in her eyes. "I don't understand. What is the little robot saying?"

"We're elected."

* * * *

As they exited the dust cloud, Karen stayed on the bridge and asked if the poachers were following. "Our sensors were damaged in the attack and we cannot detect anything beyond a thousand kilometers of this ship," it answered. "We shall have to hope that they have gone elsewhere."

"Can't you contact those eel men like you did before?" she asked.

Guider spun left then right. "It is unlikely that they would fall for your ruse again. Calling them and informing them that they would find a prize on the surface of Delberon was indeed genius."

It *had* been a good idea. Blaron was greedy and she was sure that the other poachers were as well, so having them kill each other off first—she remembered the phrase 'thinning the herd'—had been a good idea at the time.

However, Guider was right. They wouldn't fall for that trick again. She also knew that Blaron wouldn't give up so easily. He wanted revenge like an alcoholic wanted a drink. Still, they continued on and a few hours later landed on Larjas Seven.

At the entrance, Guider appeared and informed them, "We do not have much time. We cannot be sure if the poachers are following us or not. We are sure, though, that the time you spend here must be extremely short."

Let's get on with it. "What does this tallonium look like?"

"The rock is a light blue, much the same as the color of your sky on Earth, and we need only about twenty pieces."

"You're sure that you can, uh, convert it?"

"You have seen the engines and our technology, Karen," the little ball answered. "Once you have the tallonium, bring it to the engine room, and we shall do the rest."

Karen felt uneasy about handling something like this. Her chemistry teacher had made them study the periodic table and words like plutonium and radium jumped out at her. "Uh, I don't want to sound like a wimp, but is this stuff safe? I mean, it's not radioactive, is it?"

Guider bobbed up and down. "No, it is only toxic if received in large doses and with continued exposure, that being measured in months, not minutes. We must hurry. The ore is light and will be easy to carry once you get it from the mine."

"A mine," Karen repeated, shrugging. Well, no one told her this would be easy. "Okay, we'll get in and out fast. Tell me about the air."

"It is somewhat thin, but breathable."

Since their mission was clear, Karen motioned to the exit, and Ralus crept behind her fearfully. "Will we be okay?" she asked.

Telling her the truth would have been the plan, but dealing with a little kid called for a white lie. Karen didn't know what else to say outside of, "I have no idea."

The doors opened and they gazed upon a desert-like world, filled with stones ranging from shoe-sized doorstoppers to immense boulders the size of semis. Sand was everywhere, and a fierce, cold wind whipped through the area, hurling bits of stone and sand into their faces. Ralus' teeth began to chatter, probably more from fear than cold, Karen figured, and right now she wasn't feeling too brave herself.

"Where's the mine?" she asked Guider.

"It is approximately three hundred feet straight ahead."

As they walked down the gangplank, Ralus darted glances at the landscape and whispered that she didn't like this place. "I don't know what a mine is, and I don't want to leave the ship."

"It's, uh, like a hole in the side of a mountain," Karen told her, trying to simplify matters as much as possible. "It's a hole in the mountain then you go down into the earth and dig for rocks and gems and things like that."

Ralus didn't respond. Instead, a whimper came out of her mouth. "But the bad men might be there!"

"I know!" Karen exploded, then, regretting her outburst, kept her voice as level as possible. The kid was scared and she didn't need any extra fear enforcement.

Taking Ralus' hand in hers, she pulled her along. "I'm sorry for yelling. I'm scared, too. Listen, this is going to be easy. All we have to do is go into the mine, grab the ore, get out of there and go back to the ship. It'll take fifteen minutes, so let's get it done."

The younger girl gulped and nodded, wiping the hair away from her eyes. "I will help."

As they walked along, Karen kept her eyes peeled, just in case the poacher gang decided to show up and ruin things as usual. She wasn't sure if they knew the location of this place or had already gone somewhere else, but she figured that Blaron wouldn't give up. He had the men, he had the weapons, and he also had murder on his mind…

"Is that what we are looking for?" Ralus asked, interrupting her thoughts.

Karen peered through the screen of silt, an opening in the face of what looked to be a small mountain loomed ahead. "Yeah, that seems to be it."

Going a few paces farther, Karen saw a large, roughly hewn doorway open up into darkness. Cautiously approaching it, Karen squinted and searched for shadows, patterns of movement, but saw nothing. "C'mon," she urged, and pointed at the entrance. "Let's go inside."

Once past the threshold, the wind died away, and they walked along a narrow corridor. The place resembled Earth mines with stone walls, dampness and a smell of uncirculated air. Lights had been strung overhead, glowing orange bulbs that sent threatening shadows dancing across their path. Their footsteps echoed hollowly as they trod down a well-worn walkway, and a few minutes later, they reached the end of the passageway.

"So...where is everything?" Karen murmured.

"Over here, look!" Ralus urged and pointed with her finger.

Training her eyes in the direction that Ralus had indicated, Karen saw a narrow opening in the ground, perhaps a foot wide. Next to it sat two large buckets, one of which had a heavy rope attached to it. In turn, the other end of the rope was attached to a winch with a large handle used for cranking.

Karen peered into the hole. Yes, just as Guider had said, a number of sky blue rocks sat directly below them, roughly twenty feet down. The area was brightly lit, and a number of tools lay scattered about. The miners had probably quit this place in a hurry.

Problem number one — and it was a biggie — jumped out at her right away. The bucket would fit through the opening, but when Karen got down on her butt and tried to slip through it was a no go. She wouldn't fit. This hole had been designed for small crabs, not for large bipeds.

Shaking all over, Ralus edged to the hole, peered down and turned back with a petrified look on her face. "You cannot fit." She swallowed hard, but solemnly proclaimed, "I am smaller than you are. I'll go."

Oh...this was a disaster waiting to happen, but they had no other choice. Karen ground her teeth together and made a decision. "Okay, I'll lower you in the bucket and you toss the ore inside. Then I'll pull it up. Once you're done, we're out of here."

Ralus clung to the sides as Karen winched her down. Her muscles screamed as she strained to lower the bucket, sweat poured down her face, but she continued to crank, and soon the smaller girl touched down and gave the rope a sharp yank. "I'm here," Ralus called up. "I'll fill it."

"Hurry up," Karen cautioned, panting for air. She nervously darted looks around the cavern and made a perfunctory search for the enemy, but they never showed. Every sound, real or imagined, the plinking sound of water dripping from overhead, and scratching of whatever animals or reptiles or insects or whatever lived on this world, practically caused her to have a major panic attack. It didn't take much of an imagination to figure out how Ralus must be feeling.

Five nerve-wracking minutes later, she heard, "I'm done," from below.

Bringing up the bucket, she emptied out the rocks into the second bucket, knocked out the dust, and lowered it. "Okay, get in and I'll pull you up."

She waited for an answer, but the dead air whispered in her ear that something had to be wrong, and her feelings of uneasiness grew.

"Hey," she called down softly. "Can you hear me? Is something wrong?"

No one answered, but a second later she heard a sharp cry that abruptly cut off. A spear of terror knifed through her.

"Ralus!" she yelled. "Are you okay?"

Silence followed then she heard a scratching sound, followed by the heavy thud of footsteps, a sound she'd come to know and hate.

"Karen Fox, I must assume that you are up there?" a familiar voice called out.

Blaron! How did he...? When she peered into the hole, Karen could see the large man filled the space below. His horrid looking face wore an obscenely cheerful grin, as if he'd discovered the secrets of the universe.

"Hello there," he called out. "We meet yet again! Would you like to see your little friend?"

Karen's heart began to beat very fast and it sounded like thunder in her ears. *Oh God, he wouldn't do that.* Voice trembling, she asked, "Where's Ralus?"

"Oh, do you mean this thing?" replied Blaron in a faux-pleasant manner. Underneath the pleasantness, though, an edge of menace lurked. "Here she is."

With his meaty hand, he held her body up by the neck. Her head dangled loosely, and Karen was alternately horrified by the sight and pissed off by the thought of this...*thing*...killing a little kid. Her gorge rose and she wanted to puke, but she held it in check. "You killed her?"

"Her neck wasn't very strong," he answered in a tone devoid of pity or any other emotion, save anger. With a flick of his wrist, he tossed her corpse away.

Oh God, no, he did it. He actually did it. Karen flattened her back against the wall, sweat pouring from her head and soaking her body. Her heart raced a million miles a second. Why...what kind of warped person would do something like this? There were rules and the rules said that you didn't kill innocent kids. Blaron had executed Ralus as if she'd been some sort of criminal.

No, it had nothing to do with justice, she decided. This was infinitely worse. He'd done it for the fun of it, because he could. He'd already murdered an entire planet, so what was one more life to him? Leaning over to peer into the hole, she lost it and screamed, "You are scum! You didn't have to kill her!"

Even in the dim light, she saw that the cheerfulness had disappeared from his face. Now, only meanness and avarice remained. "Remember, Karen Fox, you were the one who murdered my kin. Consider us even!"

He turned away, bent over to pick up something then spun back, now holding a long tube. "Wait, I have one more present for you."

As he shouldered the tube, Karen realized that it was a weapon. It looked just like a bazooka, and in a moment of terror she scrambled away.

"Goodbye, Karen Fox," she heard him cry out.

A second later, she heard a soft puffing sound, and a small cylindrical projectile rocketed through the hole, hit the ceiling and bounced down to her position.

"Oh crap," she blurted. With a quick motion, she grabbed the projectile and threw it down the hole. A second later it went off. The concussion tossed her and the bucket against the far wall and she banged into it hip first, falling painfully onto her chest. The contents of the bucket scattered along the mine's floor. Bruised all over, she felt grateful to be alive.

Dust came up through the hole, and with a sense of satisfaction, she hoped that he'd been torn apart. Getting to her feet, she cautiously moved to the edge of the hole and listened. Luck wasn't on her side. Cries of pain along with a number of curses filtered up to her position.

Hastily gathering the ore and sticking it back in the bucket, she got up and staggered down the passageway out of the mine and into the fury of the wind. It was still blowing up something fierce, and she limped back to the ship as fast as she could, grunting as she lugged the precious cargo with her and all the while fighting back tears of rage.

Once on board, she made her way down to the engine room. Guider met her there. "Was your mission successful?" it enquired. "Where is Ralus?"

Karen didn't answer right away. Instead, she stood near the main reactor shield, heaving in breaths and trying to get a handle on what had just happened. She couldn't, though, and broke down. Sobbing, she got out, "They were waiting for us. They killed her."

A moment of silence followed, and the Guider intoned in a somber voice, "We grieve with you, Karen Fox."

She wailed at the unfairness of it all. There'd been no reason for it, no reason, just like her parents had been killed for no reason.

And in that moment of self-reflection, she thought about the empty promise she'd made to Ralus about finding her a place to live. All the girl had ever wanted was somewhere to sleep and start a new life. What about all the hopes and dreams she'd had? Ralus had simply wanted to be with friends — and now she never would.

The thought of some nameless and faceless people saying that they grieved with her made Karen feel ill. What did they know? She choked up and said, "Fine, you grieve with me. Now tell me where to put these rocks. After that, you can leave me alone."

Guider hovered silently then flew down to her side. "We are sorry, Karen," it repeated. "Please, go to your left and you will see the Injection Vent. Deposit the ore in there, and the ship will do the rest."

Nodding dully, tears streaming down her face, Karen found the vent, dumped the rocks inside, and went back to her cabin. Inside, she wiped her face, stripped off her uniform and went to the shower, where she stood under the rocketing hot water until every bit of dirt had been blasted from her body. The tears kept coming. She'd had no way of retrieving Ralus' body in order to give her a decent burial. "You don't kill kids," she raged aloud. "You don't!"

Karen then realized that Blaron wasn't a person anymore. Maybe he never had been, and her thoughts turned to vengeance. Once she got dry, she changed into a pair of sweatpants and a hoodie. Lying down in bed, she tried to shut out the images of the past hour and couldn't. There'd been nothing that she could have done, but all the same, she vowed to do something from now on. She only hoped that Ralus' death had been mercifully quick.

* * * *

"Uuh!"

Karen started out of her uneasy sleep. The memory of her friend's murder came through in living color and the tears trailed down Karen's face. Her sobs of loss then turned to growls of anger, and a feeling of rage flowed through her body. Uttering a string of curses at Blaron's viciousness, she muttered, "Oh yes, there will be payback."

Ralus had been way too young and she'd been the last of her kind. Now, her planet was truly dead. If Karen had her way, she'd put Blaron in the category of non-existence as well.

Suddenly the monkey alarm went off and she started. "Guider, what's going on?"

It appeared at her side. "You have been asleep for only three hours. I am sorry to tell you, Karen, but we are being followed. We managed to get the long-range sensors online for a short time before the system failed entirely, but I have detected Blaron's ship. He will be upon us soon."

A stab of fear went through Karen's heart, but she forced the fear down. "What other good news do you have?" she asked, attempting to find some humor where none was possible.

Apparently, Guider still hadn't developed a sense of the ridiculous, as it said, "Repairs have been expedited on the star-drive conversion system, but we can move only at three-quarter speed. Additionally, our ventilation system has been compromised, and our shield's power is only at eighty percent, and—"

"Never mind," Karen said tiredly, rubbing her forehead. "So we're low on power, low on air for me and the animals, not much defense…how far away are we from your home world?"

Guider flew directly in front of her. "We are roughly thirty minutes away."

She was about to do a happy dance when the first concussion hit, a shockwave that tossed her into the wall. She slammed into it and yelped in agony. "Ouch. Was that what I thought it was?"

"Apparently," Guider said, "we have company."

It would pick this time to use an old Earth phrase. Karen thought about what to do, and a sense of resolve filled her. Jerking her thumb at the door, she commanded, "Let's go see what they want."

Chapter Twelve
Faceoff

As they made their way to the lift, more shots hit the ship and it continued to rock back and forth, nearly jolting Karen off her feet. She remembered watching an old Star Trek show and the camera always tilted at a crazy angle whenever the enemy hit the Enterprise with an energy ray or whatever they called it. This wasn't much different, except that it was real and very close.

As if reading her mind, Guider said, "Blaron's ship is very close. Without sensors, we can only estimate the distance, but we would judge them to be—"

"Screw how far they are!" Karen yelled, frightened and angry, and sweating heavily. "Don't you have screens up or something?"

"We have protective shielding," Guider answered, "but it will not last long against their weaponry. They are using some kind of plasma array, and—"

"Save it!"

This was no time for a lecture on interstellar weaponry. Struggling to her feet, she wondered aloud, "What would a captain do in this situation?"

"We are open to suggestions," Guider said.

Deciding that someone had to do something, she pointed in the direction of the wall. "Let's get to the main bridge."

Luckily, the lifts still worked, and she reached the command deck in less than ten seconds. Guider waited at her side, hovering just above her right shoulder, and she limped over to glance at the main screen.

Oh…this was not good. The poacher's vessel hung off the port bow, its cannons pointed directly at their ship. The light at the edge of the main view screen blinked madly. It indicated that the enemy wanted to communicate. "We are being hailed," said Guider with a note of doubt in its voice. "We must answer."

After she pressed the button, Blaron's voice and image filled the bridge. "You are to surrender, girl. We know you have no weaponry capable of damaging our ship. We know that you are weak and that you have no backup. No one is coming to help you."

"Go to hell!" she snarled. "You're not getting in!"

"I think we are."

More shots followed, rocking the ship from side to side, and Karen got thrown to the floor. "We are under attack," Guider said. "They mean to destroy this ship, or at least cripple it."

"They're doing a good job," she muttered as she picked herself up and in a moment of weakness, whispered, "What should I do?"

Silence ensued. "They want the menagerie," Guider finally answered. "However, all life is precious. Your life is valuable as well."

Nice to know, she considered as another shot rocked the ship. The yellow light flashed once more and another shockwave, this one harder, tossed her against the wall. Blaron's voice, sounded more world-weary than ever and it echoed over the bridge. "That was your last warning, Karen Fox. We have the capability and the means to decimate a planet. Our next salvo will blow your ship apart. Open your bay doors and let us in."

Making a quick decision, Karen turned to Guider. "Let them in." She pressed the button to cut off the transmission and Blaron's face faded from view.

"As you have commanded, the doors to the bay are opening." Three seconds later, it asked, "Do you have a plan?"

She thought quickly and got to her feet. "I've got an idea. You told me before about the emergency escape pods for the animals, right?"

"We use a different term than your people do," Guider answered. "But yes, we have them, and they are operational. However, if you remember, they can only be used in close proximity to a planet."

"Are we close enough to yours?"

Guider hummed, and when it spoke, it sounded surprised. "We are just within range."

Mind working overtime, Karen ordered, "All right, once Blaron's gang enters, eject all the escape capsules except for the Malurian dragons. The mother's with her baby and all that moving around isn't good for them."

"It shall be as you say," Guider replied.

Making her way down to the landing bay, she found a ship the size of a commercial airplane sitting in the hangar. It wasn't as impressive as their main ship, but it was still pretty close. Twenty pig-men stood around it, all holding weapons, long-barreled guns, and she didn't want to see them up close and personal.

"Yawr," a familiar voice bleated.

As she looked down, the tolop sat there with a lonesome expression on its face and its eyes wide and clicking open and shut rapidly. "What are you doing here?" she whispered fiercely as she bent down to pick it up. "You should be hiding."

Giving it a quick tummy rub, Karen ducked behind a ship and listened as Blaron gave the order to fan out and capture her. *Not happening.* As she turned to go, she inadvertently kicked a small box. The poachers looked in the direction of the noise and Blaron yelled, "It's her! Get her!"

"Time to go," she said, and moved to the wall as fast as her legs could take her. A touch, it opened and she backed away. Good, she'd be safe for now. She had to think like an animal. The difference was, she had a human's intelligence and knew the ship's layout. The enemy didn't.

It appeared that Karen had spoken too soon, as the wall began to smoke and a red beam shot through it, nearly cutting her head off. She ducked, but not in time as burst of energy came through and lanced the left side of her face. Fire flashed through every single nerve ending she possessed and she screamed, putting her hand up to cover the injured area. Fighting back the pain, she shouted "We have to go!" and took off, holding on to the tolop.

Running over to the next wall, she got through and this time, the wall behind her exploded. Five men poured in after her and she ran as fast as possible to a far wall, touched it, and remembered that this was one of the sealed-off sections. But the opposition didn't have to know that. "Guider," she whispered.

It appeared immediately. "Yes, Karen?"

"What's behind this wall?"

"Nothing," Guider responded. "It is a void."

Oh....that was a plan. "Open it up."

The door slid open and Guider vanished. Karen took a deep breath and ducked inside, holding the tolop close to her. She waited by the side of the door, and when the men poured in headlong, she ducked outside and yelled, "Seal it off."

In a flash, the door slid shut. She heard the men beating on the door and felt absolutely no pity as she took off down a side passage. More shouts came her way, and a section of the wall blew in, taking her off her feet. She tried the same tactic on another wall, but this time the poachers didn't take the bait.

She couldn't hold her breath forever. "Guider," she yelled, "Get me out of here!"

The orb appeared and let her out of a rear door. In the hallway, she heaved in great gulps of air, and after getting her breath back, she noticed that the tolop's eyes were now glittering. Whether it was from fear or anger, she couldn't tell, but she rubbed its tummy and whispered, "Hang on. We're getting out of here."

A shout came her way. They'd found her. The tolop let out a bleat and Karen hustled over to the elevator, but not before a laser blast speared its way through the wall and sliced into her right leg. She fell hard, landed on her bad leg and screamed in agony. The shot had cut through the clothing on her right leg and taken out a chunk of flesh. Fire blazed through her muscles, searing her brain in the process.

"She's over there!" one of the poachers cried. "Get her!"

This was most definitely not good. Breathing heavily now, she hauled her butt into the lift and made her way down to the enclosures, hiding behind one of the larger structures. As far as she could tell, almost all of them were empty. Good, the animals would be safe now. Rounding a corner, she found the poachers there, armed to the teeth and spoiling for a fight.

Blaron spotted her and called out a cheery greeting. "Karen Fox, it is so good of you to welcome us aboard!" He executed a series of gestures and his men fanned out, trying to encircle and entrap her.

"Screw your welcome."

She backed up slowly, pushing the tolop behind her. It started to growl, a sound she'd never heard before, something low and hoarse and guttural, and something totally alien to its usual way of expressing itself. "Shh," she whispered, and rubbed its stomach. It didn't mewl this time, though. Instead, its voice simply dropped a few decibels and it kept growling.

Up ahead, Blaron ordered his men to stop and put their guns down. "I have asked my men to take heed of their surroundings," he said in an amiable tone. "I do not wish to damage anything on this ship. Not only does it carry valuable cargo, it also carries technology as well as additional ships for the menagerie. Loss of life means loss of money for me and my crew, but I will not hesitate to destroy what is necessary."

Of course it would be all about screwing up his profit margin. Heart racing, she took in a series of deep breaths to steady herself. Her right leg still hurt from getting shot and her face burned as if someone had lit a flare against her skin, but she could still stand and wouldn't go down without a fight. Not now. "You're trespassing," she stated. "Get off this ship."

Her opponents laughed, their voices echoing across the park. Blaron stepped forward, the expression on his face a mixture of amusement and menace. "Girl, listen to me very carefully," he said, right eye twitching. "You have been a pain in my side since Delberon. You have caused me to lose men, time and most of all, profit, and you will not stop me. Stand aside and let me take what is mine."

"You won't find them. They're gone."

Blaron's jaw sagged and he stopped dead in his tracks. "What do you mean they are gone?"

"If you have sensors or something, check for any departures from this ship headed toward the planet nearby."

He stared at her a second before snapping his fingers. One of his men handed him a cellphone-sized device. Blaron read it, his lips moving soundlessly. A second later, his mouth began to twitch as did his hands, almost as if he had the shakes, and he dropped the device. "You little witch! You sent the animals away!"

"I did," she declared, and couldn't help but offer a smile of triumph. "They're probably already on the planet below us and I know you can't get through their defenses."

His right eye began to twitch again, faster this time, and he let out a snarl. "You know of our weaknesses. No matter. There are still two species left here. I will take them as compensation."

"No."

Karen kept backing up until she reached the wall. Stealing a quick glance over her shoulder, she noted the location of the triangle, and put her right finger behind her back. Touching the wall gently, it opened up, but the tolop didn't run inside. It merely hid behind a barrel and Karen cursed the little creature's devotion to her.

Blaron heaved an exaggerated sigh and rubbed the burned side of his face. "You are forcing me to lose my patience, girl. Stand aside and you shall not be hurt."

"Get lost."

With Karen's declaration, his right eye went full twitch mode and he lost whatever decent manners he'd had in the first place. "We want them!" he screamed. "Do you comprehend the words that I am emitting from my mouth? We want them!"

"Can't have 'em."

It hurt to move, but after getting to her feet, her bad leg trailing behind her, she made her way over to the door of the enclosure. The Malurian dragon was there, baying and head-butting the door and she knew that he wanted out. The poachers, though, weren't willing to give up their chance.

"Listen to me, girl," Blaron said, his voice sounding weary as well as exasperated. "You are outnumbered, outgunned and outclassed. You cannot even walk and I do not care if you have a bad leg. You simply have to move aside and walk away."

As Karen's hand found the door, he laughed. "Or shall I say, limp away."

His joke caused the other men to laugh with him, but they didn't see what was coming their way and had no reason to. Poachers had to be as dumb as a bag of rocks. They knew how to steal, but they didn't know what they were stealing...and they knew nothing about the various species on board. Knowledge was indeed a dangerous thing.

Karen touched the door and it opened. She snapped her fingers and the male dragon stomped out, his eyes red and blinking from the sunlight. His mate hung back, with her baby peeking out from behind her. Guider appeared at her elbow. "Karen, you must leave."

"Not happening," she answered. "Not..."

A blast from Blaron's gun hit Guider squarely, spun it around and it vanished. "That made for good target practice." His men roared with laughter.

Now truly pissed, Karen reached inside the enclosure and took out the sunglasses. "Funny you should mention target practice," she said. "I was thinking the same thing." She placed the sunglasses over the dragon's eyes.

The chortling quickly stopped as the dragon's skin turned yellow. She swung herself on his back with a practiced move and getting a hold of the loose scales near the nape of his neck as makeshift reins, she tapped him between his ears. He responded by snorting and pawing the ground. "Hey, guys," she called out. "Let's rumble!"

And now came the definite and long-awaited *oh crap* moment. Every single poacher stared with their mouth open, waiting for orders. Too late, though, as Karen lifted the sunglasses, the dragon's instincts kicked in and it charged.

Blaron did the only thing he could do. He scampered away, leaving one of his men as a very convenient target. The Malurian dragon's rush literally destroyed him as its razor sharp teeth tore him in two. Mass screaming broke out as the animal zigzagged with blinding speed in spite of his size, and each stomp of his paw or head-butt broke or mangled an offending trespasser's limb.

Two minutes and twenty scumbags later, most of the other thieves had scattered. They were still there, though, and a shot came from over a rise and hit the dragon squarely between his eyes. He collapsed with a groan and threw Karen off. She landed hard on her injured leg and screamed from the impact.

Crawling beside him, she petted his head. "Hey," she whispered, "are you okay?" She listened carefully. He was still breathing. "You pigs!" she screamed.

A laugh from Blaron came her way. "The animal is only unconscious," he called back. "It would do us no good to bring back a dead body. Our sponsors want their pets alive!"

Another shot hit the dirt in front of her and chewed up a sizable chunk of turf. "That, on the other hand, was a warning," Blaron continued. "My sponsors are not interested in a keeper of a menagerie. However, personally speaking, you are young and I still consider you pretty outside of your infirmities. You would make a fine mate for me, so I reiterate my offer. Stand aside and let us have what is ours. If you do not accede to our wishes, then you will soon be dead. Make a choice!"

Scrambling for cover, Karen hid behind a rock, her breath coming out in short gasps. Part of her wanted to vomit in fear, while the other part wanted to vomit at the idea of this monster touching her. Even his breath smelled like a sewer. She had only one choice, and that was to protect the animals. If these pirates captured her, they'd kill her, anyway, and her injured leg had begun to bleed. If she didn't die from blood loss, then she'd die at their hands. She made a silent vow to kill herself and as many of them as she could take with her if they tried to violate her.

Ripping off a piece of her uniform and tying a makeshift bandage around her leg, she stifled a scream as the fabric bit into the wound. Another shot whizzed over her head.

"Girl, you are making me angry!"

"You're making me sick!"

Taking a deep breath, she got ready and made a break for the main door. Two feet in front of her goal, she felt something smack her squarely between the shoulder blades and she tumbled head first into the wall.

Dazed, she watched as they approached guns in hand, and the lead poacher bent over to examine the dragon. He briefly patted the fallen animal on its side then straightened up with a sigh. "Girl, I must commend you on your loyalty to the Keepmasters and the precious cargo they carry, but it has all been for naught. We have the men, we have the animals and we have you."

A grin split his porcine face, showing off his nasty, rotting teeth. "However, I have decided to take back my generous offer. I prefer whole women."

Raising his gun, he aimed it at her, and Karen, while thoroughly terrified, decided to meet her end with honor. "Go ahead and do it," she uttered in what she figured was her final moment of defiance.

"Yawr!" a voice to her right called out. "*Yawr!*"

Turning her head around, she saw that the tolop had arisen, balancing on two of its tentacles. While it still looked cute and cuddly, the look in its eyes portended otherwise. Gone was the gentle expression. A look of rage stood in its place.

Blaron's look of superiority vanished and a note of uncertainty entered his voice. "Why is that animal...? It did not act this way on Delberon or Ansar."

"It was scared then," Karen replied with a touch of wonder. "It's not now."

With a quick shove of one of its tentacles, the tolop pushed Karen out of the way and inhaled deeply, quickly expanding to two, then five then twenty times its size. Its tentacles formed into gigantic six-toed feet, stomping over to where Blaron and his men stood gaping in terror. "*Yawr!*" it screamed, and its voice caused the entire compound to shake and Karen's eardrums to vibrate.

Blaron and his gang took a step backward, another, then with a cry of fear they began to run. It didn't do them any good, as the tolop's body flowed over them, enveloping them and trapping them inside it. Now Karen understood why this species didn't have any natural enemies. She heard the muffled screams of the men as they tried to punch and kick their way out, but soon the screaming stopped, as did their movements.

Only Blaron remained, cowering and covering his head with his arms. Stiffly, Karen got to her feet and limped over to where he sat, shivering. His weapon lay at his side and perhaps he could have fired it at her, but he took no notice of it.

"Nice job, tolop," she said. "Nice job."

Blaron seemed to recover his senses somewhat and reached for his weapon. Karen bent over, quickly snatched it away and rammed the barrel against his head. "Give me one good reason why I shouldn't blow your head off," she snarled. "You murdered a little girl's planet, you murdered her, and you wanted to kill me, too." She smashed him on his uninjured cheek with the barrel, shredding his skin, and he howled with pain. "Go on and tell me!"

"You're a nice young lady," he said, eyes pleading for mercy. It was just an act, though, and he made a grab for the weapon.

Her finger twitched and the gun went off, atomizing his head.

"I've learned not to be."

Sick at what she'd done, she let the gun sag in her hands but didn't drop it. Even though Blaron had deserved it, did her actions make her any better? Maybe and maybe not, but she'd deal with the guilt later on. Another job had to be done first.

Pivoting around to face the tolop and patting it on one of its tentacles, she pointed at the far wall. "If everyone inside you is still alive, let them out. We're going to the Landing Bay."

A second later, every poacher flew out of the tolop's body, and it shrank to its normal size while the poachers lay on the ground, frightened and gasping for air. Karen trained the gun on them and ordered them to stand up. "Your leader, what's left of him, is lying there." She motioned with the weapon to the corpse. "Make one attempt-to-be-a-badass flinch and I'll do the same to you. Now move it!"

Silently, they did as she commanded, and once inside the Landing Bay, she ordered them into one of the ships used to transport the alien animals. As the men filed in, one of them asked, "What...what are you going to do to us?"

"We're going to send you on vacation," she answered. "Guider," she called out, and the little ball appeared. It moved erratically in the air, though, and its voice sounded somewhat unsteady, the volume fading in and out.

"Yes, Karen?" it asked.

"Can you program this vessel to go anywhere?"

The ball bobbed up and down, but its words came out disjointed. "It...done...can do...be done."

"Send them somewhere very far away, somewhere cold, and somewhere where they'll never come back," she said.

The man who'd spoken to her made a desperate grab for the gun, but she let loose with a mighty swat and smashed him squarely between his eyes. He collapsed in a heap and she slid the door shut. "Have a nice trip," she stated.

Limping outside with the tolop cradled in her arms, Karen saw Guider throw up a video of the inside of the landing bay. Karen watched as the cargo bay doors opened and the vessel lifted off. The doors shut. It was over.

Well, almost over. The ship was still damaged, and with the adrenaline rush fading, her leg was really starting to hurt now, along with her cheek, her shoulder and everything else. Weakness hit and hit hard, and she slumped against the wall, but refused to sit. If she sat down then she wouldn't be getting up again.

"Guider," she grunted, "how bad is the damage? Can we make to your home planet?"

"We are...unsure. Our engines...at only seventy percent capacity...our shielding is almost gone." It paused and wobbled, and its voice grew fainter. "We are entering the atmosphere now."

As if on cue, the ship began to shudder and the tolop whimpered. "Close off all unnecessary compartments and give the power to the shields," she ordered. "The enclosure...the animals we have...put the spare shielding around them. I'm going there now."

"Command received," Guider said very faintly. "This communication instrument has been...irreparably damaged by the enemy. You must...get to the enclosures...can eject them."

"I'm staying."

"You must...leave..." Sparks suddenly flew from its body. It emitted a brief squawk, fell to the ground and lay still.

Karen's head lolled and she felt faint. Losing blood, she knew, could do that to a person. The tolop put its head against her chest and she rubbed its belly as the ship continued to shudder and shake.

With a massive effort, she limped over to the elevator and reached the enclosures a few seconds later. The Malurian dragons were baying in fear, so she went inside in order to do what was necessary. She didn't want them to be alone.

"Hey," she managed to get out as she stroked the iron-hard skin of the male. "Hang tight. We're almost there."

She flopped down on the ground between the two larger animals, and the baby settled against its mother, whimpering. The tolop said nothing, but it started to expand once more, spreading its limbs and its body around her and the dragons.

The shuddering continued, and the ship shook so hard she thought it would break apart. Half-conscious from the blood loss and general exhaustion, Karen heard a loud bang and she felt the ship hit something hard. It bounced once then again, and had she not been held in the tolop's embrace, she would have been smashed against the walls.

As it was, she merely got jolted, but the jolts were way stronger than just making her teeth shake. She felt like every bone was about to fly out of her body and screamed for help. The ship continued to roll forward, but it was slowing down, slowing…then it stopped.

"That," she said weakly, "was one giant ride."

Karen fell over onto her side and the tolop seemed to cry and shrank back to its usual small state. She reached out to rub its stomach. "It's okay," she whispered. "I think we got you back."

A grunt came from inside the enclosure. It was the male dragon, and he seemed to be all right. A lighter voice sounded. That was the female, and a moment later Karen heard the trumpeting sound of the baby. Good…they'd made it.

Darkness began to fill her field of view, but before it completely overtook her, she heard a voice call out, "We are here! Karen Fox, please show your face. You are safe now."

Digging down into the last reserves of her strength, Karen raised her hand and managed to cough out, "This way!"

Then the pain became too much to bear. Still, she had a sense of triumph. The menagerie was safe. They were safe. It had been worth it.

"I'm over here," she called out again.

"We are coming."

Swiveling her neck around in the direction of the voice, her triumph turned to terror as something reached out for her with a craggy, bony hand. It couldn't be true, but her eyes, blood covering them aside, beheld an image of a being well over ten feet in height, green-skinned, with a head that looked like a cross between a demon and a rabid dog. She blinked the blood out of her eyes and saw extremely long fangs, no nose and tiny horns protruding from its temples.

Then she lapsed into the well of unconsciousness, wondering if this was the end. Just before the fade-out happened, she managed to say, "Can you feed the canarians?"

They didn't like to go a day without food.

E p i l o g u e
All is revealed

Waking up in a semi-darkened room with shadows crisscrossing the floor, Karen found herself lying on a bed of soft cushions. Someone had taken off her bloody uniform and dressed her in a loose-fitting gown. Was this a hospital room? It didn't look like one — not really. Other than the four unadorned walls, the only thing that she saw was a square mirror affixed to the wall across from her.

She'd had a dream, that of a massive demonic being reaching out to her, lifting her up and carrying her off. She smelled nothing, but felt its powerful hands cradling her gently, felt its warm breath upon her then…nothing. Although she tried to speak, no words came out, and the being didn't communicate with her. Then the dream faded and she entered a void.

Now back to the land of the conscious, she felt her body all over from head to toe, and her fingers encountered a bandage on the upper left side of her face. A sudden, sick feeling flowed through her. *It's another scar. It has to be. Well, at least both sides match.*

Resigned to the inevitability of it all, she sat up, swung her legs over the side of the bed, and carefully stood up and started the trek over to the far wall. After three steps, she stopped and blurted out, "What the...?"

Her right leg...it felt normal. This wasn't possible — couldn't be possible — but testing it, bending her leg at the knee, she experienced no pain and no weakness. Someone had obviously repaired the damage, and pulling up the side of her gown, even in the dim light she saw that it matched the left, lean and muscular and no trace of damage. It was as if it had never been injured at all.

Her right arm also felt normal, and she saw whole, untouched and smooth, clear flesh. Karen's hopes rose as she walked over to the mirror.

Hope then turned to disappointment. She hadn't seen her face for so long, and she was certain that whoever had fixed her leg and arm had also taken that horrid mark away.

Reality, though, didn't lie, and the image she saw brought her back into the here and now. Her hair, tousled and filthy, hung limply down to her shoulders. She'd only been gone around ten days, but so much had changed. The look in her eyes, though, the smudge of black mixed in with the green, remained.

In a moment of weakness, Karen knew it was all about vanity. While the scar on the right side of her face was still there, she wondered about the opposite side. When she gently peeled off the bandage, she found another livid mark ran from her hairline down to one inch below her left eye. Tears started to pour down her face and she put her hands up to her mouth, hoping against hope that this was all a bad dream.

"I knew it would happen like this," she whispered. Her fingers slowly put the bandage back, but after deciding there was no reason to hide the truth, she ripped it off and tossed it to the floor.

"Do all your people litter?" a voice asked from the far corner of the room.

Whirling around, she saw a figure standing in the shadows. Tall and wide, it resembled the figure from her dream. A demon coupled with a dog, fangs and all — that's what she'd seen. "We do not have bins for waste on our world," it said, but from the manner in which it spoke, it sounded like a mild rebuke.

"You're telling me not to litter?"

Thoroughly angered and heartsick at her appearance, she mustered up all the defiance she could and balled her fists. "Okay, I just faced off against a group of poachers and kicked their butts with some help, so if you're going to kill me, then take your best shot."

"Why would we wish to kill you?"

The voice, deep and harsh, but with an oddly gentle male quality to it, jarred her. Did all beings from the Lower Depths speak this way? Listening to the timber of the voice, it was harsh, but for some reason it sounded very familiar. "Who are you?" she asked.

Her visitor stooped over to pick up the bandage. She saw that he was wearing a long overcoat of some sort, breeches and high boots similar to hip waders. "My name is Hallan," he finally said after putting the bandage in his pocket. "I am the leader of the Keepmasters. You are on Jiggeku, my home world. This is a care center, what you on your planet would call a hospital."

Karen took a moment to collect her thoughts. "Did you fix my leg?"

"Correct."

Her head snapped up. The way he'd pronounced the word *correct*...this was the voice of Guider back on the collection vessel! After deciding to wait on this bit of revelation for a moment, she asked him, "Why?"

Silence for a time then, "If you mean repairing the damage to your leg and to your arm, it is because you wished it. When you first spoke to us on our transportation vessel, you mentioned your infirmity. We did not know of your ailment nor did we understand your physiology, not entirely. It was only after further research that we learned of how to heal nerve damage that occurs in your race. Some scars, however, still remain."

There were some other scars that couldn't heal, those upon the psyche and soul, and Karen wondered if these people had taken that into consideration. Maybe they had and maybe they didn't know or think it worthwhile.

"What about my face?" she asked. "Can you fix that, too?"

More silence followed, and then he answered in a quiet, measured tone, "No."

"No?"

"We are sorry. The damage that was done to you in your initial accident back on your home world, along with the damage done to you by the poachers is irreparable. There are some things that even our technology is not capable of. In your case, the nerves in the injured areas of your face were completely severed."

Karen heard the explanation, but the one word that stood out was irreparable? No, it couldn't be, and she started to cry. One side of her face was bad enough, but now she looked like the Joker, minus the white makeup and permanent grin. "You can't...can't make me look normal?"

"We are sorry."

She sat down then, legs tucked under her body, and sobs racked her, making her stomach shake and her muscles quiver with tension and fear and self-loathing. Hallan remained a monolith, quiet and unspeaking. Finally he asked, "Is appearance so important to your people?"

Karen heard his question and continued to cry. She managed to sob out, "You read my thoughts. You know that I lost my family and all my friends because I got sliced up. How would you feel if you were ugly? What do you know about being...being hideous?"

"We know."

Hallan reached behind him and touched the wall. The room lit up and he stood there, just like in her dream, a vision of hell come to life. His eyes were a demonic red, and his fangs were indeed sharp and wicked looking things, yet when he spoke again, his voice sounded disarmingly gentle. "An image we saw in your mind, Karen Fox, an image of a mythical creature your people have nightmares of?"

"Oh God," Karen gasped and scuttled backward until she reached the opposite wall. Thoughts of what might happen next collided in her mind, but from the way he spoke and how he calmly stood there without so much as moving a muscle, it was plain to see that he didn't want to hurt her. He remained in his part of the room, hands, horned and craggy, clasped in front of his body. "This is…"

"Yes, this is how we look." He answered her unspoken question in a very calm and unruffled manner. "Is our appearance so distasteful to you?"

Her lips trembled. "I…" Her voice trailed off. "I've never seen anyone like you before," she answered truthfully.

"Yet perhaps you think of us as not being your ideal, is that not so?"

Karen didn't answer, but deep down she knew what he meant. This alien knew her better than she knew herself. "Yes," she finally managed to say.

"Come with me," he said, motioning to the far wall with his hand. "You are free to walk outside. I will show you our world."

He went to the wall on her left and pressed a triangle. The wall parted down the center. Hesitant at first, Karen summoned up her courage and walked out alongside him into the bright sunlight. The air here was slightly heavier than that of Earth, but it didn't present any immediate problems. Her focus centered on the world that lay before her.

In a sight that forced a gasp from her, she took in the nature that filled the immediate area. Trees, oddly shaped bluish-gray things that stood as tall as telephone poles, resembled mushrooms but only in the vaguest way. A smell not unlike cedar drifted over and she inhaled it. It had a calming effect on her system and she felt her body relax. Hallan gestured with one massive arm to a destination off to their left. "Let us go."

As they strolled along, Karen wondered if she should have anything covering her feet, but found that the walkway was a soft kind of metal that yielded under her body weight and massaged the soles of her feet. *This is incredible. How can they do that?*

Oh wait. They were aliens who had superior technology. They could make foot massagers. They could build interstellar ships. They could probably speak a million different languages. So why couldn't they fix her face? A few tears slipped from her eyes and she hurriedly wiped them away.

Numerous other beings like Hallan—she wondered in a moment of the ridiculous if they were called Jiggekans or Jiggekians—passed them by. They also wore similar clothing and bobbed their heads in a friendly manner. None of them remarked on Karen's mode of dress or anything else, although they did glance at her, more out of curiosity than with loathing, she considered.

Swiveling her neck around, Karen could see immensely tall glass buildings standing off in the distance, and overhead, metal craft hummed by, along with some multi-winged, brightly colored birds. A riot of emotions flowed through her and she had a million questions. "This is your world?" she asked. "Where exactly are we?"

Hallan gave a brief laugh. "It is obvious that you have many questions. I will try to answer them. We are in our capital city, Melvok. Our planet is in a distant part of the universe, so far from your point of origin that even your most powerful instruments cannot measure the distance. We belong to an alliance of no less than four hundred worlds. However, it was not always this way."

Intrigued, Karen asked, fumbling for the right words, "How is...I mean, what happened?"

Her host waved his hand at the buildings in the distance. "As we explained briefly while you were on our containment vessel, years ago our world was torn by war. It started before I was born and continued on until only recently. I am approximately twenty-eight of your years old, the way your people calculate age. Most of the planets in this sector of the galaxy, as well as the adjacent ones, warred among each other for twice that period of time."

"Why?"

He offered a shrug. "Expansion, was, is, and always shall be the blight of sentient beings, a scourge on our so-called intelligence. Interplanetary expansion, mineral and ore rights, and claims of racial superiority, among others, were the reasons for the conflict...I imagine that your planet suffers from the same problems."

Social Studies and American History classes had told her the same story. "Yeah, it does."

Hallan continued to speak quietly. "For us, the result of the conflict was an incalculable loss of life for all our people. The war devastated the economies and ecologies of the planets in our galaxy.

"Finally, after years of unceasing war, the leaders of our worlds signed a peace treaty. However, a problem soon surfaced. The ecologies of the other worlds had been so damaged by the bombings and subsequent fires that many species among their animal populations were practically decimated. They were in danger of dying out."

Hallan clasped his hands behind his back, and his voice took on the tone of a professor delivering a lecture to rapt university students.

"As our world is ideally suited to most species and the fact that we have superior technology in many areas, we volunteered to host their animals, keep them safe and help to breed them. Once they have been bred and their populations increased to the point of no danger of extinction, we will return their offspring to their home worlds."

They turned a corner and came to a grove of trees. "This way" — he gestured with his arm — "our safe spot is not far from here."

Continuing their walk, Karen began to feel more at ease, not only because her leg didn't bother her anymore, but also due to the fact that this alien — and then she realized that *she* was the alien in this setting — spoke to her as an equal, not as a teenager. "Ah, we have arrived," Hallan said, an air of satisfaction lacing every word. "This is what I wished to show you."

Karen let out a slow exhalation and a smile formed on her face. It hurt her newly injured cheek, but right now she didn't care. She faced an open zoo, much like the one on the ship, but infinitely larger. Many of the animals and life forms she'd taken care of were walking around, some of them free to roam and others behind clear glass walls. They seemed calm enough, but when the tolop spotted her, it let out a loud, "Yawr," and ran over as fast as its tentacles could carry it. Hopping into her arms, it purred out a wee mew of pleasure.

"Glad to see me?" she asked, comforted by its presence.

Hallan tapped her on the shoulder and pointed to her right. "Behold. Here they are, and there are more up ahead. As they demonstrated on the vessel, they are comfortable not only in each other's company but in ours as well, and they do not need the docility drugs anymore."

Pivoting around, she saw many of the menageries' inhabitants all in a row, standing or squatting or flapping their wings. Putting the tolop down, she walked over to them. "Did you miss me?"

Naturally, they couldn't talk, but they crowded around her and nuzzled her legs, licked her hands and face and let their joy at her presence be known by cawing or uttering other unearthly sounds. All three Malurian dragons wore oversized sunglasses, and they trumpeted her arrival accompanied by a loud blast of fetid air from their nostrils.

The female dragon came forward in an awkward waddle. As for the baby, it crawled out from under her and Karen knelt down to give it an obligatory head-butt.

"They seem to be fond of you," Hallan observed with a note of amusement in his voice. "They did not show as much affection for their prior keeper."

He moved off before she could answer, so Karen ran after him, saying, "Wait, guys. I'll come back!" It was a pleasure for her to run and she figured that she'd be getting in some middle-distance training soon.

Hallan walked steadily down the path until he came to a series of round metal stool-like objects. Sitting down on one of them and drawing his coat behind him, he gestured to Karen to take another, similar seat. After she did, she asked, "What's all this about affection?"

Hallan didn't speak for a time, merely looked out over the forest then back at the animals that were still waiting. "Your predecessor," he finally said, when he turned his gaze back to her, "was a refugee from one of the wars I spoke to you about earlier on. His planet had been destroyed by the conflict and his family had been killed. He had nowhere else to go."

Reaching into his pocket, he took out a square, card-shaped disc. "This is what he looked like."

A holographic image sprang up, showing a humanoid male in his early twenties with a small head, even features and gray eyes. He stood beside two other individuals, perhaps his parents, older and more lined, but with similar features. Karen gasped. "This isn't the..." And her voice suddenly cut out as the totality of it all overwhelmed her.

"You understand now, do you not?" Hallan asked in a gentle voice.

She nodded and her heart began to speed up. "He was injured in the war, wasn't he?"

"Correct."

A lump formed in her throat, and while she wanted to hold back her emotions, she couldn't and started sobbing. "No one wanted him around?"

"Correct."

Tears blinded her and she let them flow unchecked. After handing back the picture, she wiped her eyes and sniffled. "That's why you chose me. It wasn't because I was the first person you saw or the best qualified—"

Hallan held up his hand and waved it at the animals, all of whom were waiting patiently. With a casual move, he stowed the picture away and offered in the most fatherly and soothing of all voices, "When our first keeper died, we happened to be passing by your world and needed to find a suitable replacement. We originally thought of locating someone trained in the art of handling animals, but there was no time. It was simply good fortune that we landed near your care center.

"Then you happened along and found the tolop. Even someone with knowledge of animals would have been frightened, or might have tried to injure it. We watched as you approached, and knew that you were only trying to do what you felt was right."

"But...I didn't even like..."

Hallan held up his hand. "Please allow me to finish. When our instruments connected us to your mind, we saw your impressions and knew of your feelings for lower forms of life. We were aware of your past history. However, over the course of this journey, you have transcended your fear."

His face took on a more introspective expression, and his voice retained its fatherly, quiet and encouraging quality.

"Know this. An animal in a zoo or a pet in a home is not interested in the appearance of its keeper or master or mistress. It does not care about wealth or social status. It only knows voice and touch and manner. It only wishes to be fed and cared for and...*loved*. And if your values are the same as ours are — and I believe this to be true — then an animal's love for its owner is unconditional."

As Karen listened, a lump the size of a grapefruit formed in her throat, and she was incapable of speech.

"As for appearance, our race would be considered ugly or deformed or both by your planet's standards would we not?" Hallan continued.

"Correct," Karen answered, recovering her voice, then stumbled out, "I mean..."

Abruptly Hallan broke into laughter. It was a deep and rolling sound that seemed to come from the pit of his belly and spread out upon the air. He held his sides as if to contain his mirth then, after his manner sobered, his voice resumed calmly. "It is understandable. But your answer waits for you, over there."

He pointed in the direction of the animals. "You cared for them and they in turn, cared for you. They still do. I have eyes, and I can see as well as anyone."

Karen's heart now beat so fast she thought it would explode, but after taking a few breaths, she felt it slow to its normal rate and turned her gaze to the herd.

A wise look appeared in Hallan's eyes. "Recall my earlier explanation of the farmer and the gem. Do you understand now?"

Karen thought about it and made the connection. "When that farmer who found the gem...he gave it away, and the second guy gave it back and asked him to give him another gift more precious...yeah, I remember."

"The answer is obvious. You gave the gift to these animals. You gave them your love."

Karen licked suddenly dry lips and a moment later, clarity ruled. She'd seen before, but now...now it all became oh so very clear. Wiping another sudden burst of tears that had involuntarily sprung from her eyes, she jumped to her feet and stated without a second thought, "You know something? I'm fine now. I mean, I'm going to be fine."

"I do not understand." Hallan seemed surprised, his eyes growing round. "Are you talking about your appearance?"

"Yeah, that's what I meant," she answered. "I'm not worried about my looks or anything—not now."

"But...from the images we received from your mind, your emotions concerning appearance, we were under the impression that your people prize beauty above all other things. Why do you act so unconcerned?"

Karen shook her head as a rush of emotions surged through her. "I don't know really, just that—what you said—the animals like me and I like them. I mean, I'd like to look pretty just like any other girl out there, but maybe...maybe..."

Her voice trailed off, and she knew that she hadn't articulated her thoughts well, but if the animals could accept her as she was, then she had to as well. There would be moments of doubt in the days ahead, but she'd handle it. And as for anyone else, if they couldn't, then that was their problem and not hers.

Hallan merely nodded. "Perhaps I understand what you have said, Karen Fox of Earth." He arose and brushed off his greatcoat. "If you are ready, then may we make the arrangements to send you home?"

Karen started to say something, but her speech got interrupted by the tolop totter-walking over and jumping into her arms. "I think I am home," she said, nuzzling the little creature. Fortune had indeed smiled on her. At least Blaron had been right about that. "I *am* home...if that's okay with you."

Her declaration caused Hallan's mouth to drop open. "You are sure about this?"

While he seemed surprised, the corners of his mouth twitched upward in the semblance of a smile, and Karen knew that he needed her to stay. Maybe the people here had the concept of vacations, and if they did, one day she'd go back for a visit. Ron's mind would be blown at all of this. She knew that for sure, but as for everyone else...?

No, there really wasn't anyone, not anymore. While it was quite convenient for her to be alone—though she missed Ralus and always would and as for her parents, no way could anyone ever replace them—but right now, being alone didn't matter, not anymore. A second later, she came back to reality and found Hallan staring at her, a look of curiosity in his eyes.

Matching his gaze, Karen answered firmly, "Very sure. The canarians need to be fed every day, the Malurian dragons' baby needs to be cared for, too, and the tolop has to be rubbed in a certain way. If it doesn't get its way, it has a fit!"

The last part of her sentence caused Hallan's eyes to narrow with incomprehension. "I do not understand what you mean by *a fit*," he replied. "Does this mean that you are volunteering to stay on?"

"Correct."

Once more, her answer caused him to drop the façade of seriousness and his laugh practically rustled the leaves of the trees around them. "Then I shall contact my colleagues and we will find you a place to live. Since we have no more keepers as capable as you are, I find myself in the position of asking for help."

Karen knew this to be a lie. The people here were far more advanced. She had a lot still to learn, but all the same, it gratified her to know that they trusted her to do what needed to be done.

Hallan motioned with his arm to return to the waiting menagerie. "I think your friends are waiting for you. They seem anxious."

With a slight bow, he turned and strode away, and Karen ran back to where the herd was waiting eagerly. Coos and caws and grunts and more greeted her, and the tolop didn't leave her side for a moment.

"Yeah, you missed me," she whispered, finally content.

As Karen petted and stroked them, she saw a plaque that had been cemented to a stone. Its message was the same as that of the plaque in the Knowledge Repository Center.

We do this for they bring us happiness.

We do this because they have no defense, nowhere else to go, and no one to care for them.

We do this in order so that they may teach us what it means to be different, and for us to embrace that difference.

Karen intended to embrace that difference and keep it close to her for the rest of her life. Here she was now and here she would stay. The ark had landed and dry shore was hers to walk on. And while she had a lot of sightseeing and catching up to do, right now she had meals to prepare and buckets to fill.

About the Author

J.S. Frankel was born in Toronto, Canada, a good number of years ago and managed to scrape through the University of Toronto with a BA in English Literature. In 1988 he moved to Japan and started teaching ESL to anyone who would listen to him. In 1997, he married the charming Akiko Koike and their union produced two sons, Kai and Ray. J.S. Frankel makes his home in Osaka where he teaches English by day and writes by night until the wee hours of the morning.

J.S. loves to hear from readers. You can find his contact information, website details author profile page at http://www.finch-books.com.

www.ingramcontent.com/pod-product-compliance
Lightning Source LLC
Chambersburg PA
CBHW030140180626
46812CB00002B/781